SOMEONE'S IN THE KITCHEN WITH . . . JAKE

"Mom? What are you doing? Mom?"

"Hush, baby," said Jackie again. By this time Peter was wide awake. He listened to the sounds coming from downstairs—Jake's low, throaty growl, followed by deep, menacing barks.

"Jake's barking at someone in the kitchen," said Peter. "Who's in the kitchen with Jake?"

Jackie stopped trembling long enough to orient herself to the sound. Peter was right. Jake was now below them, in the kitchen. She could hear the frenzy with which he hurled himself violently against the back door, all the while keeping up his savage barking.

"Turn out the light, Peter."

Peter obeyed. Jackie went slowly to the window and looked out. A dim figure was moving swiftly through the shadows of the yard. A shiver ran through her.

Peter looked up at his mother. "Jake did a pretty good job, didn't he, Mom?"

"He sure did, Petey. He sure did."

A TAIL OF
TWO MURDERS

MELISSA CLEARY

DIAMOND BOOKS, NEW YORK

This book is a Diamond original edition, and has never
been previously published.

A TAIL OF TWO MURDERS

A Diamond Book / published by arrangement with
the author

PRINTING HISTORY
Diamond edition / July 1992

ISBN: 1-55773-738-X

Diamond Books are published by The Berkley Publishing Group,
200 Madison Avenue, New York, New York 10016.
The name "DIAMOND" and its logo are trademarks
belonging to Charter Communications, Inc.

PRINTED IN THE UNITED STATES OF AMERICA

10 9 8 7 6 5 4 3 2 1

For Alex

A TAIL OF
TWO MURDERS

CHAPTER 1

In the deserted cobblestoned street behind Leanna's Piano Parlor, in the second week in November, a man lay dead.

He was a man in his late middle years, with a grizzled face and an untidy head of thinning, yellow-gray hair. His red nose and his sagging cheeks told of a long friendship with the bottle; his expansive stomach stretched at the fabric of a cheap and stained shirt, open at the collar. His jacket was moth-eaten; his overcoat tatty. Next to him on the uneven gray cobblestones lay a well-made and well-worn fedora; it had begun to surrender its shape to the cold, mucky water of an icy puddle.

The man had an enormous wound in his chest. Later on, the Palmer medical examiner's office would determine that the weapon was a .44 Magnum; a serious handgun, the kind of weapon used by people who kill often, and deliberately.

The man's face bore a look of unmistakable surprise, as though he believed he had bought tickets to a football game, only to find himself at the opera. Or had believed himself among friends, only to discover otherwise.

At his feet sat a large Alsatian shepherd with a patient look on its face. The dog must have been grazed by a bullet; a thin, dark, spreading stain discolored his right front leg. He licked at the wound almost carelessly, his eyes on the corpse.

For a wounded dog, it was a long way from here, where there was death and danger, to the county road. The county road was not especially safe, either; but on the county road, the threat of being struck by a car was perhaps less terrifying than the prospect of remaining here, where half-wild stray dogs roamed the city streets in subtle and silent packs.

And there was always a chance that the man with the gun would come back.

With evident difficulty, the dog picked himself up and licked gingerly at his leg. Then he took a last look at the dead man and loped off into the night.

"Ahh," said Jackie Walsh, settling low into the hot, foamy water of her bath. She stretched a long, sudsy arm out of the water and reached languorously for her pristine copy of *Sophisticated Woman* magazine. The scent of the perfume ads mingled with the scent of the bath bubbles, filling the warm, moist air with a heavy sweetness that was, if not appealing, at least luxurious.

Outside, the afternoon traffic moved fitfully along on Water Street. The sound of whizzing tires and impatient horns drifted up faintly to the duplex loft and penetrated Jackie's thoughts, but she found the noise reassuring. She was a child of the city, recently come home again.

"This is living," said Jackie to herself. Using her free hand, she deftly coiled her abundant dark hair into a pony-tail; then she lay back and gazed appreciatively about her. The bathroom—like everything else in the old industrial building—had been newly renovated. She smiled happily at the gleaming chrome of the sleek Italian plumbing fixtures. She had carefully economized on almost every part of the renovation, but when it came to the bath she had lost patience with her puritanical streak and indulged herself. The bath was her one concession to the little voice within her that had urged her, since her divorce, to live it up. The indulgence, she reckoned, had been worth it.

Jackie Walsh began to relax. It had been a long day, and she still wasn't quite used to being back at work full-time.

During her lengthy married interlude in the suburbs, she had worked hard as a wife and mother; her days had been filled with trips to shopping malls and well-appointed health clubs, day-care centers, the dry cleaner, the grocery store— endlessly in and out of the car. Every evening, she had felt as though she had put in a full day's work—but after ten years, there wasn't much she could point to and say, "That's mine. I did that. I made that." There was Peter, of course— her ten-year-old son. Other than her hours and days with Peter, however, Jackie's memory conjured several thousand healthful and economical dinners, and what felt like a million loads of laundry. Nothing more. She knew that she had failed, somehow, to meet the challenge—but there it was. She *had* failed to be inventive and lively and happy in the suburbs. At least she had cut her losses. She was happy in this old building, with its exposed pipes and high ceilings and tiny backyard, facing on an alley that ran toward the waterfront.

The adjustment to professional life had been more difficult than Jackie had anticipated. But now, two full months back into teaching in the film department at Rodgers University, things were beginning to look up. And it was good, very good, to be back in Palmer again, with the old, familiar shops right on the street, and the city buses ready to take her wherever she wanted to go.

She was thrilled once more to feel herself part of a human community; the car culture of the suburbs had made her feel less than human, always strapping herself in to her four-wheeled envelope of privacy to drive from the elementary school to the donut shop to the hardware store. It was good for her soul to be back among the bustle of pedestrians, to be a party to the acrimonious give-and-take of city politics, to shake her head over the shenanigans surrounding the St. Patrick's Day parade. She was thrilled to be close, once more, to the opera and the theater and, most especially, the abundant first-run movie houses, showing films imported from Italy and France and Japan. Ah, how she had missed the movie houses, living in the suburbs. And how she loathed shopping malls!

Jackie slid farther down into the bathwater and prepared to take the *Sophisticated Woman* quiz. She didn't mind that the quiz was intended for women twenty years her junior; her recent divorce had left her curious about the world of dating—a world now strangely unfamiliar. She was aware that her ideas about love and romance must be hopelessly out-of-date.

Not that she was looking for romance. But Jackie Walsh was a woman who liked to be prepared. So she had taken to reading women's magazines; and with typical intellectual thoroughness, she read them carefully. She found *Sophisticated Woman* the silliest—and accordingly she loved it the most.

"Do You Keep Score In Love?" asked the headline. Jackie laughed, her gentle brown eyes alight with irony and pleasure. She read on.

"If your boyfriend gives you a birthday present you *really* hate, do you: (A) Smile and keep your mouth shut, then get back at him? (B) Let him know it, *gently*? (C) Laugh about it behind his back with your girlfriends?"

Jackie mused. This was not a situation she had personal knowledge of—she almost always liked the presents that people gave her.

"C," she said finally. "Definitely, C."

"Mom!" came an impatient wail from downstairs.

Jackie ignored the call, concentrating on the questions.

"Your boyfriend has gone on an important business trip to the city where his old girlfriend lives. Do you: (A) Call him every night to make sure he's in his hotel? (B) Act like you don't care, even if you're seething—then make a date of your own? (C) Send him flowers and an *intimate* note?"

"A," said Jackie to herself.

Peter pounded on the bathroom door. "Mom! Come *on*! I'm gonna be late!"

Jackie pictured him, suited up in his hockey duds, his reddish curls peeking out from under his helmet. She loathed ice hockey, but there was nothing to be done. Her boy loved it, as his father Cooper loved it. They were ice-hockey nuts, father and son. "I'll be there in a minute. Have you got your hockey stick?"

"Yeah." There was a resounding thud on the carpet outside the bathroom. "Come *on*."

"Coming," she moaned reluctantly. As she dried off, she watched the bubbles—still alive with the soothing promise of luxury—slide slowly and fitfully down the drain.

Jackie Walsh dressed quickly and piled her boy into the car. They were headed to the nearby Jaycee's rink, where Peter's team, the Mighty Mites, were playing.

"Are you sure you have everything?" asked Jackie as they pulled away from the curb. "Gloves."

"Yeah." Peter held up his gloves.

"Good. Who's going to win?" Jackie negotiated the huge five-way intersection near the National Bank tower and headed onto the six-lane highway, which cut like a gash through the heart of Palmer.

"Us. We're gonna *kill* 'em. They're dead meat."

"Are they? Glad to hear that, I suppose."

"And after the game I'm invited over to Bobby's house."

"Okay. For the night?"

"Nah, just dinner."

"Okay, that's fine. Bobby's mom going to bring you home?"

"He doesn't have a mom. Maybe you should watch the game, Mom. And then come over with me to Bobby's."

"I have to teach a class tonight, honey. You know that."

"Yeah, I know." Peter banged his hockey stick hard against the underside of the dashboard.

"Don't pout, baby. It doesn't become you."

"Yeah." Peter grinned at his mother. He privately regarded her as a kick, although he was careful not to show it. Most boys had moms that drooled all over them all the time.

Peter was enjoying his new life as a downtown kid. The ice hockey was really the only trace of suburban existence that still clung to him, after two months at the Downtown Arts School. It wasn't that he eschewed his former life—he merely, like his mother, found the city invigorating. There were always plenty of people to look at, places to go and hang out—and you didn't have to wait around for your mom or dad to drive you everywhere.

But he did miss his dad. Peter closed his eyes and tried very hard not to think of his dad.

Jackie, for all her independence and distracted air, was keenly alert to Peter's moods. She knew instantly that he was thinking about Cooper.

"Dad'll be here on Sunday for the big game," she said gently.

"Yeah," said Peter, opening his eyes and fixing his gaze firmly on the road ahead.

In the basement of the Longacre Center of Communications at Rodgers University, Jackie Walsh regarded her students seriously. They slouched in their chairs, eyes half-closed, with a self-conscious artiness that hung about them like an aura. The fashions were different, but these students were as familiar to her as if she had never left teaching.

Jackie had been arty herself, as a college student. She understood it well. There were people (her ex-husband among them) who still thought of her as terribly Bohemian; her black clothes and the downtown loft living did nothing to dispel that notion. Thank heavens her mother approved, and Peter was happy; even if her ex-husband would never understand.

The class had just finished watching *Beauty Knows No Pain,* the classic documentary-style film on Texas cheerleading. Jackie had always found the film—an ironic look at the ardent struggles of cheerleading hopefuls—moving and instructive. It was an excellent point of departure for a discussion of documentaries; next week, they would look at *Roger and Me*.

"What separates this kind of film from a true documentary?" Jackie asked the class.

"Point of view," suggested a long-haired, leather-jacketed boy in the front row.

"Right. Now, where does the point of view come from?"

"Narration?" suggested a rail-thin, blond-haired beauty with pouty lips.

The class discussion wore on, along familiar but earnest and interesting lines. Despite the predictability of the semester's curriculum, Jackie was glad to be back. And if she was lucky, she'd be able to persuade Philip Barger, the dean of the communications school, to let her try out the new course she had designed. They were scheduled for a meeting on the subject tomorrow.

Jackie brought her mind back to the subject and finished up the discussion of documentary filmmaking just as the hour was up. As she gathered her belongings, she glanced with curiosity toward an intense-looking brunette who had been seated in the back row. The young woman's name was Danielle Sherman; and according to department gossip, she was having an affair with Barger. The news was hardly shocking: Barger had an affair with a different student almost every year. Each fall he selected a student for himself, in just the way a professor might choose reading material, or perhaps with less deliberation. "Barger's Bits," the unfortunate undergraduates were labeled.

This year's selection looked bored and slightly antagonistic. She was very pretty, and a bit more sophisticated than the ones Jackie remembered from the past. Barger was probably growing more demanding in his old age: *He must be pushing fifty by now,* thought Jackie. She wasn't so far from that watershed year herself. Oh, well. At least she would never again be a temptation to Philip Barger. In the old days, he had made more than one pass at her. Jackie watched the young woman depart, then gathered up her

books and headed down the hall. Perhaps Barger was still
here; she needed to speak to him about using the editing
room tomorrow afternoon for the film lab.

Philip Barger leaned back in the luxurious brown leather
armchair at his desk. An amused look of superiority flitted
across his handsome face; he knit his full gray brows in
a parody of bemused concern, gazed distractedly at his
fingernails, and spoke once more into the telephone.

"Look—I'm sorry, but that's just the way it is. Way of
the world, my dear." He fiddled with the paperclips in a
sleek steel cylinder on his desktop; a look of bored impatience replaced the amusement, and he spoke again. "No.
I can't see you this evening, I'm afraid. Not this evening,
nor any evening in the foreseeable future. You'll just have
to live with it. Thank you so much for understanding." He
cradled the receiver and leaned back, adjusting the crease of
one trousered leg. A satisfied smile appeared on his face.

In the doorway, Jackie cleared her throat.

Barger looked in her direction. "Jackie, my dear. Come
in, come in." He gestured expansively toward the visitor's
chair across the desk, looking her up and down with an
appraising eye. He gave her a conspirator's smile and nodded toward the telephone. "The importuning litany of the
former spouse will soon be as familiar to you as it is to me.
Sit down, sit down. Have a drink."

"No, thank you, Philip," she replied demurely, remaining
firmly in the doorway. "I only came to speak to you about
the editing room. I'd like to reschedule my film lab for
tomorrow morning, if that will suit."

"I'm sure it will suit, my dear. But Polly, you know,
keeps the books on that." He shot out a wrist and glanced
at his watch. "Gone for the day. I'll tell you what. You can
have my key. Polly's is locked up. Let me just take a look
at the calendar." He rose and opened a door that led to a
small adjoining office, and Jackie could hear the rustle of
pages turning on a desk calendar. "Looks like it's all clear

tomorrow, but she's most particular. So use my key, and leave her a note, telling her I okayed it. I'll be here into the wee hours, I expect, working on the Great Undertaking."

"Ah, yes—the Grosset project." Jackie nodded. It was very big news at the Longacre Center—Philip Barger had secured the movie rights to the Kestrel trilogy of Graham Grosset, who was widely considered England's finest living novelist. Grosset had a visiting professorship at Rodgers, but he had remained distinctly aloof from his colleagues in the English department; and as far as anyone knew, he considered the rest of the faculty entirely beneath his notice. How Barger had pulled off this coup remained a mystery, and Jackie Walsh, like everyone else at Rodgers University, was curious. The word around the department was that the screenplay of the first book was nearly complete.

Jackie and her colleagues had been forced to reconsider their doubts of Barger's importance to the department. Apparently, after all of his years of behaving like a selfish and empty-headed idiot, Philip Barger was about to prove himself, and make a contribution to the body of work produced at the Longacre Center. "I hear that you've lined up Ivor Quest to direct. That's pretty impressive."

Barger smiled, reading her doubts. "Want to leave a note for Polly?" he asked, proffering pen and paper.

Jackie scribbled a hasty note. As she wrote, she could feel Barger's eyes on her, and her mind flew instantly to Danielle Sherman, the intense brunette in Film History 101. Perhaps the experience would be educational for the pretty sophomore. Jackie couldn't imagine getting involved with him—no matter how he redeemed himself with the Grosset project. But she knew better than to let her dislike show. Philip Barger was a ruthless man, in college politics as well as in romance.

Jackie handed him the note for Polly Merton, smiled, and took her leave, feeling very uneasy.

As she headed out to the faculty parking lot behind the Longacre Center, she wondered idly who it was Barger had been talking to. It hadn't been his ex-wife, Celestine. Of that, she was sure. Jackie had known Celestine Barger fairly well, in the old days, and unless the woman had had a personality transplant, there wasn't a chance she'd want to see Philip Barger. Celestine Barger had no use for her former husband.

Caught up in her speculation, Jackie almost didn't see the large brown and black dog making its slow way across the road in front of her car. She slammed on the brakes and watched, distracted, as the dog limped off into the night.

CHAPTER 2

"Mom!" called Peter Walsh from downstairs. His voice was full of anxious excitement. "Mo-om!" he insisted.

"What is it, Petey?" Jackie was behind schedule and fretful. She glanced hurriedly at the clock on her dresser—seven forty-five.

"Mom, hurry up!"

"Coming, coming," said Jackie with a sigh, tugging on her turtleneck. She made her way hastily downstairs to the kitchen, where the door to the little backyard stood open.

"Look!" said Peter, pointing.

The object of his intense scrutiny was a dog—a large, grizzled dog, with a massive head and a half-suspicious look in his eyes. He was lying on one side, two or three feet from the back stoop. As Jackie studied him, he twitched an ear and raised his head.

"Dear God," murmured Jackie.

"There's something wrong with him, Mom."

"Yes, Petey, there is indeed. Don't go near him, sweetheart."

"But he needs help. Look!" Peter pointed again, this time to the dog's right front leg, where the fur was matted with a thick, hard layer of congealed blood.

"Tell you what, Peter. You get him a bowl of water, okay?"

Peter rushed to comply, and she sat down on the small stoop to study the dog. It was a chilly morning for mid-

11

November, and the overcast sky promised rain. Jackie shook
her head. They couldn't ignore the animal.

She stretched out a hand, palm down. With evident difficulty, the dog raised himself and hobbled slowly over. He
sniffed at her hand, then looked away. She kept her hand
very still, and the dog sniffed it again.

"Cold nose, warm heart," said Jackie gently.

The dog licked her outstretched hand. She reached gently
out and scratched behind his ear.

"You're awfully handsome," she remarked as Peter
reappeared, carrying an enormous aluminum bowl filled
with water. The boy put the bowl down, and the dog
drank.

Peter stood back and watched, thoughtful. "Do you think
he's a stray, Mom?"

"Could be. He doesn't have on a collar."

"But he's awful beautiful just to be nobody's dog, don't
you think?"

"Yes, sweetie, I do."

"How do you think he got hurt?"

"In a fight, probably."

"Or maybe hit by a car," suggested Peter.

"Or maybe hit by a car," his mother agreed. She looked
at her watch. Still plenty of time before school. "Get me
the Yellow Pages, Petey."

Half an hour later, Jackie and Peter were sitting quietly outside the examination room at the office of Jason
Huckle, D.V.M. The room was filled with the scent of
dog shampoo, and there was a noisy transaction going
forth between two waiting cats, who spat at each other
from within their carry-cases while their owners looked
the other way. In a corner, a handsome, dark-haired man
sat perfectly upright, a worried look on his face and a tiny
Yorkshire terrier in his lap. "Good dog, Guido," the man
said gently, stroking the miniature dog's fur. "Good boy,
Guido." Guido sniffed, closed his eyes, and went to sleep
in his owner's lap.

Before long, Jason Huckle emerged from the examining room with the dog Peter had found on a lead.

Huckle was a tall, thin man with a handsome air and an easy, loping walk. He presented the end of the lead to Jackie.

"He'll do, Mrs. Walsh," said Huckle.

"Thank you very much for seeing us, Doctor," Jackie replied.

"No problem. It's a good thing you brought him in. He seems to have lost a lot of blood, and he's a bit disoriented. We bathed him, and I've given him a mild painkiller that will wear off in a few hours. No idea who he belongs to?"

"No. None. He simply turned up in our backyard this morning."

"Well, he'll need looking after for a short period, I would think. The city pound isn't a pleasant place to recuperate, but I feel I should recommend that you be very careful with this animal if you decide to look after him yourself."

"Oh?" Jackie looked at the dog, who bore on his handsome face the attitude of one who promises to be very, very good. She could detect no aura of wildness, or of estrangement from humans. But perhaps his benign demeanor would evaporate when the drugs wore off. "You think he might be dangerous?"

Huckle shook his head. "Not on the face of it. He seems to be a well-mannered animal. But I mended a broken bone in his leg; and if I'm not mistaken, the fracture was caused by a bullet."

"A bullet!" exclaimed Peter, looking with awe at the dog.

Guido's owner looked up in alarm, then glanced tenderly down at the Yorkie. He murmured something to the little dog, which yapped.

Huckle nodded to Peter. "I would say that this dog has been keeping rather rough company. He seems to be even-tempered, but it's obviously impossible for us to know what he's been up to. If he's been working as some kind of guard dog, he may cut up rough."

"Yes, I see," agreed Jackie. "What do you think we should do?"

The vet rubbed his neck and looked down at the dog. "Well—you say you have a backyard?"

"Only a little one," she replied.

"Is it fenced?"

She nodded. "We haven't been keeping the gate closed, though. That's how he got in."

"Well, then, perhaps you could let him stay outside in your yard for a few days. Close the gate and give him plenty of good food and water. If he wants to leave, he'll find a way out; but this will give the wound time to heal. And in the meantime, you can try to turn up the owner." Huckle leaned down and stroked the dog's head. "He is quite a beauty, for all his age and infirmities. Someone is probably looking for him now."

In the squalid alley behind Leanna's Piano Parlor, officials of the Palmer medical examiner's office were packing away their equipment. The body had been carted away; and now Cosmo Gordon, the chief medical examiner, was deep in consultation with a uniformed officer. In his hands, Gordon held the dead man's hat. He twisted it around absentmindedly as he spoke.

"Matt Dugan was murdered, Sergeant. I think we'd better find the person who's responsible."

"Yessir," replied Felix Cruz. He made a note. "I put in a call to the precinct office, as soon as you made him. You're sure it was Dugan?"

Gordon scratched his head and adjusted his glasses, glowering at the sergeant. "We worked together for many years, young man. We were friends."

"I didn't know that, sir. That is, I thought Dugan . . ."

"You thought Dugan was a disgraced ex-cop with no friends left. You're only half right." Gordon adjusted his own hat—a worn porkpie full of tiny holes where dry flies had been attached. He pulled a ratty scarf closer about his throat. "He was a good cop, once. Let that be a lesson to you."

"Right, sir." Cruz looked over his shoulder as an unmarked car approached. Lieutenant Evan Stillman was at the wheel, and Cruz breathed a sigh of relief. This was a bad situation, no doubt.

Such a swift identification of the derelict body in the alley had been mere chance. The corpse had had no wallet or papers about it; and Cosmo Gordon had only turned up at the scene because Roy Thomas, the assistant coroner, had been given the day off. Thomas would never have been able to make the body. The location and the gritty manner of the dead man's death would in all likelihood have consigned the corpse to a long, anonymous wait in the John Doe drawer at the Palmer morgue. But Gordon had turned up—and discovered his old friend Matt Dugan.

Most of the members of the Palmer force would have failed to recognize Dugan, even when he was still alive. Long before his death, he had lost the spring in his step and the set of the shoulders that had in his youth marked him as a fine police officer. Dugan's life had come tumbling down about him fifteen years before, his respectability and pride demolished by the twin demons of drink and gambling.

On the Palmer force, Dugan had no remaining contacts; nor was there any family here, as far as Gordon could remember. Dugan's ex-wife had long since departed for somewhere better—Baltimore or Philadelphia, or somewhere. Gordon couldn't remember. She had taken the children, and Dugan had descended farther and farther into a world of rough players and unforgiving habits.

But Cosmo Gordon had occasionally still seen Dugan— once every few years. Oddly enough, Gordon had seen him only three weeks ago. Dugan had appeared at Gordon's door at the dinner hour and been received like an honored guest by Nancy and Cosmo. After a good supper—much needed, as far as Gordon could tell—he and Matt had strolled out along Elmhurst Road, in the respectable suburb where the Gordons lived, to the city bus stop at a nearby shopping center. There the two old friends had sat, quietly waiting in the cool air of an October evening. Dugan appeared to have something on his mind, but Gordon had been only half heeding his old friend's rambling conversation. He wondered now, in the face of this untidy death, if he ought to have listened more closely. This was a terrible way to die, and no mistake.

Evan Stillman had finished listening to Cruz's report on the body. He strode over and shook Gordon's hand. "Well, well, Doctor," he said, "I guess no one will be surprised at the way this one turned out."

"Hello, Evan," said Gordon. Evan Stillman was too young ever to have served with Matt Dugan. The tales that had come down to the younger members of the force were cautionary and filled with disdain for the once-illustrious policeman who had fallen from grace. Drink and debt, debt and drink—and the temptation to enhance the slim salary of a cop with the ready offerings of the unclean city executives, merchants, and mobsters who ran outside the interests of the law. Stillman had no way of knowing that Matt Dugan had once had about him the promise of greatness. "Terrible," was all Gordon could say.

"Don't suppose we'll turn up much here," replied Stillman. "The forensics boys will be by, but it doesn't look to me like there's much in the way of evidence. Just a clean shoot."

"Yeah," agreed Gordon. "A clean shoot."

"He was a pal of yours, wasn't he?"

"Long time ago, really," replied Gordon evasively. He didn't want to try to explain to this man the strength of that old bond. He doubted Stillman would understand.

Evan Stillman had a reputation for doing everything by the book, with no sidetracking and no exceptions. His goal was to make twenty years with an unblemished record—

rapid promotions, a clean logbook, and no room for loose ends. At the end of twenty years, there was the pension, and golf, and probably Florida.

Gordon knew that Stillman was a good cop, the kind who would never come off the rails—the kind who would never have a chance of glimpsing, much less understanding, the tortuous ways of the human spirit. An enviable state of mind, Gordon often thought. The reasons, the compulsions, and the passions that drove people to break the law were not within Stillman's powers of comprehension. Stillman had made lieutenant, but Gordon doubted he'd ever make captain. He lacked imagination, which was the key to being a great cop. Matt Dugan had been a great cop, with too much imagination.

"I don't think we'll get far," repeated Stillman. "But I'll put a couple of uniforms on it."

"Right," replied Gordon. He headed toward his car.

"Doctor," said Stillman. Gordon turned. "The hat, Doctor. I think we had better hang on to Dugan's hat, for now."

Gordon looked down in surprise. He still held the dead man's worn fedora in his hands. He turned it over to the lieutenant. "Find the bastard, Stillman," said Gordon.

At nine-thirty that morning, a harried Jackie Walsh took from her pocket the keys that Barger had given her and headed for the editing room. She made her way swiftly down the corridor, keys jangling in her hand, wondering if she had done the right thing in bringing her small boy to live in the city.

Peter, naturally, had fallen in love with the wounded dog. Jackie wasn't sure she could handle the heartbreak that was certain to follow, one way or another. Maybe they would find the owner, and then could get themselves another dog. A real dog, a dog for them, not a stray watchdog that had been shot up on the city streets.

For the first time since their move in September, Jackie

allowed herself to focus on the violence that was a natural part of life in the city. Of course, the danger had always been a consideration, but in all her years of living here, she had never felt threatened. In the main, Palmer was a peaceful place, and the isolation she had felt in her suburban living had seemed to her a more palpable threat to the health and happiness of her small boy. Today, however, she felt that the city had begun to let her down.

She forced these concerns from her mind as she reached the end of the corridor. She recognized the figure of David Surtees, a young instructor in the department, standing before the door. He jangled a set of keys at her.

"Are you scheduled for the room this morning, Jackie? Polly told me it was free."

"Good morning, David. Well—I wasn't scheduled, but I was hoping to reconfigure things and bring my Film History 101 in here this morning. Scheduling conflicts."

Surtees put the key in the lock and turned. "I only came by to pick up some tapes from the strongbox. Be out of your way in a jiffy."

He pushed open the large, solid wooden door. Within, all was darkness; in the gloom, the familiar shapes of the huge machines seemed to lurk in uneasy anticipation of the morning's activities.

Jackie reached for the light switch on the wall, and overhead the long fluorescent tubes flickered unevenly for a few moments before filling the room with a hard, white light.

The room was crowded with masses of equipment. Against the wall were four large splicing decks, shrouded in see-through plastic covers. There were dollies, booms, and hand trucks lined up in haphazard rows against the wall on the right, and at the front of the room was a large locker where the cameras and videotapes were kept.

"I won't be a second," said Surtees. He started into the room and stopped suddenly in his tracks. "Jackie," he said, pointing with a shaking hand.

Jackie stepped forward and looked.

The body of a man lay facedown on the cold cement floor. She knew at once that it was Philip Barger. His body was awkwardly aligned, his feet pointing at impossible angles, and his right arm behind him in a position that must be painful. If he could feel it.

"Jesus," Surtees swore softly. "It's Barger." He seemed frozen to the spot.

Jackie took a deep breath and approached. She felt Barger's right temple with the back of her hand: icy cold. She fished a small mirror from her purse and placed it, with a trembling hand, before Barger's nose. No condensation. Dead.

There was a faint, foamy trace about his lips that had a sinister untidiness to it. Why hadn't he wiped it away?

"Is he okay?" Surtees asked in a shaking voice.

What a morning, thought Jackie Walsh.

CHAPTER 3

"Can't we keep him, Mom?" asked Peter predictably. They were in the kitchen; Jackie was making a pot of spaghetti for supper, and Peter was hard at work making lost dog notices. "I mean, let's put a limit. I can put it right on the sign—'If you do not come in two weeks, we will keep the dog.'"

"Sounds like a dog-napping ransom note to me," replied his mother. She had had a very long day. After discovering Barger in the editing room, she had canceled her classes and waited while the campus security forces came. They were followed by paramedics, who were in turn followed by more security forces.

Most of the day had been taken up with interviews with the chief of security, a man called Hupfelt. He was a large man with a prominent belly and thin, greasy black hair. He gave Jackie the creeps. Hupfelt was sure that Barger had died of a heart attack; that he had gone into the editing room to do something—review something, put a tape away—and had been overcome.

Jackie Walsh had seen enough movies to know that such a suggestion was nonsense. In vain she protested about the switched-off lights, and Barger's key, in her possession. She left the long interview session feeling frustrated and annoyed; but she suspected that before long there might be another opinion. Until that time, she was content to wait and to relax with Peter. Although she had disliked Barger, she had harbored no wish to see him dead. And it was very clear to her that something about his death had been dreadfully wrong.

Peter didn't notice his mother's distracted air, and he chattered on, unperturbed. "I think two weeks is fair, don't you? I mean, if nobody comes to get Hero in two weeks, then they don't deserve him. Right, Mom?"

"Hero?" asked Jackie.

"I think that's a good name. He *looks* like a Hero."

"Does he? I had thought we ought to call him Fritz."

"Fritz?" retorted Peter, disbelieving. "Fritz isn't a name for this dog. Fritz is a name for a schnauzer."

"Well—this one's a German shepherd."

"No. An Alsatian. That's what Isaac says." Isaac Cook was Peter's new friend at school; and Isaac, as Jackie knew only too well, had three dogs. Isaac had paid a call after school, to pass judgment on Peter's dog.

"Yes, I suppose Isaac qualifies as an expert, in a way." She stirred the spaghetti sauce. "What's the difference between a German shepherd and an Alsatian shepherd?"

"Size, coloration, and country of origin," recited Peter. "This breed comes from Alsatia."

"Alsace," she corrected, not at all sure about Peter's information. "Alsace is a region on the border between France and Germany, traditionally under dispute." She thought a moment. "Well—you can call him whatever you like, but Hero sounds like a made-up dog name to me."

"Hmm." Peter pondered this. Above all, it was important to give a dog a name that had the ring of authenticity. "You think so?"

"Well—yes. Like a dog in a dog-food commercial—the kind where the white-haired man tells you, 'Old Hero here eats nothing but Sloppo. And just look at him.' And you know perfectly well that the dog isn't really called Hero.

His real name is something like Champion Don Quixote of the Windmills, only his owners just call him Pancho or Fleas."

Peter chuckled, bent in concentration over his lettering. "Can I put a time limit on, Mom? Two weeks."

"Suppose Hero's owners have gone away for *three* weeks, Petey? Don't you think Hero should be the judge of how much time is enough time?"

"Well—if they just kind of *turn up,* after maybe a month, then he might have forgotten all about them. He'll want to stay with us."

Uh-oh, thought Jackie. "He might or he might not, Peter. We don't know what kind of a life he's had. I bet he's at least ten years old. What if he's been wandering for ten years? He won't want to stay."

"He will. He'll love it here. We do." Peter grinned at his mother, and she grinned back.

"Suppertime, sweetie. Clear all that stuff off the table, will you? We shall see what we shall see. Hero is his own master, I think. But we have to think up a better name for him, as long as he's our guest."

"Our guest," Peter repeated solemnly, clearing up his sign-making supplies.

The phone rang as they were finishing their meal.

"Mrs. Walsh?" asked a man's voice.

"Yes?"

"Lieutenant McGowan, Palmer police."

"Ah, yes," she replied with a look at Peter. She hadn't yet told her son about the rest of her morning. The acquisition of a dog—even a stray, even a short-term guest of a dog—was a big event in the life of a boy. The dead body in the editing room might pale by comparison. "I have been expecting your call."

"Who is it, Mom? Is it somebody about Hero?"

"No, honey. Do me a favor—run upstairs while I talk. It's business. All right?" She returned to the call. "What can I do for you, Lieutenant?"

"I'm afraid I'm going to need a statement from you, Mrs. Walsh."

"Oh? I gave a statement to Campus Security—Mr. Hupfelt."

"Yes, we've got that, ma'am, but it looks to me as though it might need some touching up. Would it be convenient if I came around to your house this evening?"

"Certainly. We're at 32 Isabella Lane."

"Yes, I know. I'll be there in twenty minutes."

Lieutenant McGowan, when he arrived, proved to be a tall, dark-haired, blue-eyed man in his early forties. He was well built and had an air of easy authority and intelligence that Jackie found refreshing. She had expected someone with a uniform, and guns, and a badge on his shirt, but McGowan was comfortably dressed in khakis and a short ski jacket over a turtleneck sweater. He showed her his identification, and she led the way into the kitchen, where she and Peter had eaten their hasty dinner.

"This is my son, Peter," said Jackie. "Peter, meet Lieutenant McGowan."

"Hiya," said Peter. "Are you here about Hero?"

"No, honey. Someone at school died this morning, and—"

"Died? You mean, like, dead? Did somebody shoot him?"

"Nobody shot him." She rolled her eyes. "Television," she said to McGowan, then turned once more to Peter. "I was the first one to find out that he had died, and so the lieutenant needs to ask me some questions. Okay?"

"Can I stay?" asked Peter.

"No. You have your homework to do, and then bedtime. I'll be up."

"Okay," said Peter. He handed the lieutenant one of his carefully hand-lettered signs. "Maybe you can take one of these and put it up somewhere? It's about our dog. Well, he's not really our dog. He's lost, and we don't know where his owners are, so I made some signs."

"A stray. He's staying in our backyard," put in Jackie.

"I see," replied the lieutenant. He read the sign and nodded approval. "It seems to cover what we need. I'll put it up in the precinct house."

"Great. Thanks."

Peter headed upstairs, and Jackie and McGowan settled down at the table to talk.

The detective pulled a notebook from his coat pocket.

"Would you like a cup of coffee?" asked Jackie. She felt fidgety, in need of something to do.

"Sure—that would be great. Cream, no sugar."

She fiddled with the coffee maker while McGowan flipped ostentatiously through the pages of a small notebook. She had begun to feel nervous about her role in the morning's drama.

"Hupfelt reported to us that you and Surtees found the door to the room locked. Did you expect Surtees to be there to let you in?"

"No," replied Jackie thoughtfully. "I had Barger's own key. But maybe I should start at the beginning for you."

With the coffee brewed, she settled in at the kitchen table and related her conversation with Barger on the previous evening.

The detective listened in silence, without interrupting, as Jackie talked. When she got to the end, McGowan leaned back and sized her up. His next words indicated that he thought she could be trusted. "I think you might be interested to know that the medical examiner suspects poison," he said without preamble. "Cyanide. We'll know for certain within the next day."

"Cyanide?" Jackie was amazed. "Hmm. I thought cyanide made you kind of—kind of sick."

"It can. Apparently this was a very large dose, and it took him fast. It was administered in something Barger had had to drink. A sweet liqueur, by the looks of it, that he kept in his office."

"Oh. Yes—that hazelnut thing."

"Almond. It had an almond flavor, which of course would mask, to some extent, the taste of the poison."

"God. He offered me a drink last night. Yikes." She shivered.

"A drink of his almond liqueur? Did you see the bottle?"

Jackie shook her head. "No. I didn't. But everyone knew he kept a lot of booze in a little cabinet behind his desk. Not a cabinet. A *credenza*." Jackie smiled. "He was a pretentious, man, Lieutenant. He always called it a credenza. It turned into a department joke, in a way."

There was a pause. McGowan looked at her steadily, then spoke. "It doesn't sound as though you liked him."

Jackie shook her head. "Nope. Nobody really much liked him. He was ruthless, and high on himself, and a little bit stupid. More than a little bit."

"And yet he was department chairman?"

"I rest my case," replied Jackie with a laugh. McGowan missed the point. "That was a joke. Kind of an academic's joke. Department chairs come in for a lot of criticism."

"The victim rose to the level of his incompetence, you mean."

"Exactly," agreed Jackie, nodding and tossing back her thick black curls. "The chairmanship was the perfect post for Barger. We could let him have the big office, and Polly Merton—no doubt you've met Polly, our department secretary—and all the fancy furniture he wanted. And that way we pretty much kept him out of everyone's hair."

"Did he do a good job?"

"Oh—no. He was a terrible administrator, and had no understanding of film. None at all. He never took an interest in a project or a thesis unless he thought he'd get some kind of recognition out of it."

"Terrific. Sounds like the mayor."

"Good comparison," said Jackie with a smile. "But Barger was impressive when you first met him, and he could handle the trustees and people like that very well. It was only when you got close to him that you could sense his limitations. So most of us just worked around him. He wasn't much of a liability, really—just dead wood." The blood drained from her face. "Bad choice of words, I guess."

"Funny how those people seem to find a job at the top."

"Well—they're no good down on the lower levels where the work really gets done. The logical place to kick them is upstairs." She looked carefully at McGowan. "Sorry. I know you're not supposed to speak ill of the dead."

"You wouldn't get very far trying to convince me that you liked him. Anyway—your honesty is kind of refreshing." He took a slow sip of his coffee and gazed at Jackie. "Any idea on who else might have had a key to that room?"

She shook her head. "It's funny—but I happen to know that Polly's key was locked away. And I had Barger's. Officially, those were the only ones. But I don't suppose it would have been too much trouble to make a duplicate; and Polly is always rather fussy about scheduling time and letting you in. I could imagine that there might be a spare floating around out there. An unauthorized spare."

McGowan nodded. The same idea had obviously occurred to him. "But you don't know for certain?"

"No."

"You say Barger planned to work late. On this big project of his, I presume?"

"I think so. That's what he led me to believe, anyway."

"Tell me about the project."

"The Grosset film. It was a surprise to us all, really, when we found out. You've heard of Graham Grosset?"

"The novelist. I liked *Napoleon at Moscow,* but not a whole lot. Wordy."

"Oh!" Jackie was obliged to give Lieutenant McGowan a second look. "I like *The Tale of Gorgonzola* best, myself.

But anyway—the Kestrel trilogy, about the obsessive architect in the Renaissance who has a withered arm and tries to murder the Pope—you know those books?"

"Sure. Passionate evil incarnate. My ex-wife's favorite topic."

"Ah," said Jackie. "Well—Grosset is teaching at Rodgers this year. A visiting lecturer in the English department. He's really more famous for being a recluse than anything else, so we were lucky to get him. I guess he needed the money—because he hasn't published anything in fifteen years. Somehow Barger talked him into a complicated deal—with him, the university, and some production company—for a movie based on the Kestrel books."

"Isn't that sort of a commercial product for a college film department? I thought you all served up Art with a capital A."

"Well—Grosset *did* win the Hodgman Prize for the series."

"Oh—so the movie is *literary*."

"Exactly." Jackie grinned.

"On the one hand, Barger had no interest in film, and on the other hand, he had this great film project going. Which is right?"

"Both, sort of. Getting the Grosset deal was a real coup, and I think there was going to be some big money coming into the university from some of the people behind it. The money people. Plus, Barger had gotten Ivor Quest lined up to direct. You know who he is?"

"Heard of him, I guess. Maybe. Hell—no. No idea." McGowan grinned. "I'm only educated for a cop, by cop standards. I'm not what you'd call one of your intellectual types."

Jackie returned his smile. "Well, don't feel so bad. He's very famous, but only famous to certain people. Very much an Artist with a capital A. So we arty types approved of the project, you see, without really changing our minds about Barger. He was going to get plenty of attention, which is what he liked. The university was getting some money, which the trustees always like. And the department was getting Ivor Quest, at least for meetings with Barger. There was even a chance of lining up some kind of lecture series with Quest. For once, Philip Barger was making everybody happy."

"Not everybody. No." McGowan sipped the last of his coffee. "Any ideas, Mrs. Walsh?"

Jackie shook her head. "Afraid not."

"You told me that you needed to reschedule your time in the editing lab. Any particular reason for that?"

"Yes—Peter has an important hockey match tomorrow afternoon. One of the teaching assistants is taking my class tomorrow, but I wanted to do the lab, which was scheduled for tomorrow, originally. I switched it so the TA could do the lecture tomorrow."

"An amazing coincidence."

"I don't see why." Jackie furrowed her brow. "Someone was bound to find him, sooner or later."

"Yes—but the killer obviously didn't realize that Barger had taken that key off his ring and given it to you. The office set was locked up in Polly Merton's desk. Polly found everything in order this morning, with no sign of tampering."

"Hmm. The door to that room locks when it shuts, but it can be opened from the inside." Jackie looked at McGowan thoughtfully.

"Yes, we noticed that. But your having the key from Barger's ring means that all we have to do is find the person with the duplicate."

"Needle in a haystack?"

"Maybe, maybe not. It depends on the lock, and the locksmiths in the area. Some locksmiths have a very good memory for individual keys. Especially when cutting a duplicate requires attention—which this would. It's a Hinsch lock—takes a special template, and duplicates are less common. And—stroke of luck—they have to be registered with the Hinsch company, for insurance reasons. So we may be able to find something out."

"Well, that's a start. Right?"

"Right. We owe it to you, Mrs. Walsh. Any chance of a refill?" He held out his cup, smiling disarmingly. Jackie filled his cup while he went on. "I understand that you teach the introductory course—film history and basic techniques. That right?"

She nodded.

"I have spoken to one or two of your colleagues. In particular, Merida Green."

"Ah."

"Ms. Green is distressed, of course, by Barger's death. But she was quite amazingly forthcoming on the subject of his adventures in life."

"Aha."

"Exactly—aha," said McGowan with a smile. "I gather that your late chairman had a way with women."

"I think it would be more accurate to say that he had a way with *young* women. Girls, even. Many college women are still girls, in terms of romance."

"What do you know about his ex-wife?"

"Celestine."

"That's right, Celestine."

"Well—I used to know her fairly well. I taught at Rodgers for several years—almost twelve years ago. She and I were friendly, then. The marriage had broken up several years before, and I didn't detect any bitterness. Well—"

"Yes?"

"Except on the score of unfaithful husbands. But that was only natural, given the circumstances."

"Which were?"

"Philip's affairs. He had plenty of affairs, even then. I don't know what was wrong with the man. It was almost a compulsion, it seemed to me at the time. I expected, when I returned to teaching, that middle age might have settled him down."

"Had it?"

Jackie felt uncomfortable. She had heard the rumors about Danielle Sherman, that much was true. But this policeman would just have to dig the dirt out for himself. "I really couldn't say, Lieutenant. I for one can't imagine getting involved with Barger in the first place, so don't ask me."

McGowan studied her for a moment, and decided not to press it.

Jackie was almost sorry that she had been reticent; her discretion seemed to have put an end to the conversation, and she was by now fully intrigued. Barger had been poisoned—by someone who knew his habits, knew that he would be working late, and had a key to the editing lab. It was a sobering assortment of facts, and Jackie had rather enjoyed her tête-à-tête with McGowan. Well—there was still plenty of time for indiscretion. She could size up the situation between Danielle and Barger tomorrow, with a little luck; and perhaps find time for another conversation with the pleasing Lieutenant McGowan.

When McGowan had departed, and Peter was safely tucked away in bed for the night, Jackie donned a comfortable old hand-woven jacket—one that she and Cooper had bought together on their honeymoon in Peru—and stepped out into the small backyard.

The dog was asleep, but he woke at her approach. She stood with her hands in her pockets, looking down at him, then squatted down on the stoop. The dog got up and limped over to her, then sat down and gave her an expectant look.

"Hi there, old fellow," she said. She stroked his head and scratched him behind the ears. "I wonder what happened to you. The doctor told me it was a bullet. Did you get into trouble with some crooks?"

The dog rested his long nose heavily on her knee, and she rubbed the top of his head softly. She kept her voice low as she talked to him, of this and that—of her marriage, and its ending, and the little boy upstairs asleep. It was a chilly night, but the dog was warm, and his nearness kept the chill at bay.

She looked up at the moon, half full and riding high behind thin clouds. She thought about the events of the day, and finally seemed to come to a conclusion. She rose and gathered her jacket tightly about her; the dog looked up, all attention.

"Maybe you are a guard dog," she said to him, "and maybe we could use some fierce protection. Heaven knows you look fierce enough."

The dog gave a low *woof.*

"Right. I think maybe the kitchen is the place for you tonight. Come on."

She opened the door and let the dog in.

In the bright light of the kitchen, the animal's black and brown coat gleamed, still magnificent from his bath earlier in the day.

He sniffed around the kitchen floor carefully for a few moments before settling himself comfortably beneath the kitchen table. Jackie reached down and gave him one last scratch, then turned out the light, closed the kitchen door, and headed upstairs.

Her son Peter wasn't the only one in danger of falling in love with this dog.

CHAPTER 4

When Jackie arrived at her office the next morning, pandemonium reigned at the Longacre Center. Usually she was among the first to arrive; getting Peter ready for school in the mornings assured her of an early start. But this morning, there was already a sizable group congregated in the faculty lounge, drinking bad instant coffee and munching on doughnuts that someone had thought to provide. A large sign, taped to the hot-water urn, advised of a departmental meeting at noon. Jackie could tell, by the length of the notice and the careful way the information had been printed on the department's laser printer, that Polly Merton was its author. *It is in the best interests of the department that ALL faculty members and graduate students attend,* she read.

"There she is," said someone as Jackie dropped her bag on a chair and headed for the coffeepot. As she fixed herself a cup of coffee, she was conscious of eyes on her. At last Mark Freeman, the animation specialist, detached himself from a group and came over to her. He was a short man, handsome, with a meticulous air at odds with his warm, friendly face.

"Well, well," he began in a hearty tone. "How does it feel to be the discoverer of a corpse?"

"Please, Mark," said Jackie.

"Sorry. Can't help being a little curious, you know. We

all are. Polly won't say a word about anything, and we feel *very* left out. Totally in the dark."

"Mark." Jackie glared at him. She liked Mark Freeman, but he sometimes came on a bit strong. All those hours spent alone in the painstaking creation of painted characters had made him unused to the company of flesh-and-blood types, she supposed.

"Well, you've got to admit it's a topic. At last we all have a subject of common interest for our next meeting."

"Yes, I suppose we do." Departmental meetings were enormously dull, as a rule. Everyone talked about what interested him, and nobody else ever listened. This lack of commonality made for brief meetings, at least—except when there were hot administrative issues before the group, such as the purchase of the new photocopying machine. That had taken up at least four meetings' worth of time, she recalled.

"Won't you say anything about it at all? Merton is absolutely mute, although she seems to have been interviewed already by the press."

"You're joking!"

Freeman shook his head and reached behind Jackie, producing a copy of the morning's *Chronicle*. "We made the front page of the metropolitan section. Look."

Jackie read the article. It was short, but to the point:

Philip Barger, a professor of film and communications at Rodgers University, was found dead in a campus facility this morning, apparently the victim of cyanide poisoning. Campus security forces, headed by Walter Hupfelt, described the death as an accident, but Palmer detectives have ruled the fatality a homicide. Lieutenant Michael McGowan, in charge of the case, would not divulge if there is yet a suspect in the crime. Polly Merton, the spokeswoman for the department, declined to comment.

"Spokeswoman?" asked Jackie.

"I found that rather amusing. Didn't you, Merida?" Freeman turned to speak to Merida Green, a woman in her mid-fifties who had joined them. Merida Green had been the first female member of the department, and she had never quite come down from that experience. She gave lengthy, well-rehearsed lectures on Film and Society—her scholarship loosely grounded in film history, which she knew well, blended with a thoroughly unsound grasp of sociological principles. Jackie had always found her awful, but she was careful never to show it. Merida was a Voice on the campus, and her courses were enormously popular.

Merida Green adjusted her gray hair, which grew in a thicket and reached almost to her waist, and spoke. "God knows Polly Merton isn't suited to be the department's spokeswoman. I can't think why anybody would have interviewed her in the first place."

"Because—there she was. They couldn't help themselves, really, if she was answering the phone," Mark pointed out. "By the way—where were *you* day before yesterday, Merida? When all the fun was going on?"

"I had to go to Boston, if you insist. For a meeting of Women in Film." She looked darkly at Jackie. "It is *high time* you joined, Jackie. It's the single most important professional association—"

"Oh, Merida, I'm just not organized enough to have time for that sort of thing." Jackie was tired of being badgered on this subject. Once a month, Merida made a pilgrimage to the association's meetings in Boston, and she was irked by Jackie's steady refusals to accompany her. Jackie had been to one such meeting, and she ardently believed that there was nothing more deadly than a group of women professionals sitting around telling each other that they were women professionals. She kept her opinion to herself, naturally, but Mark Freeman could guess at her feelings. He smirked at her comically, and she fished desperately for a new topic of conversation.

"We've found a dog, Peter and I," she said at last.

"A dog?" Merida raised her eyebrows. "How thrilling. I have a seminar. You must excuse me." She gathered up a pile of papers and stalked away.

"What kind of dog?" Mark asked with a laugh when Merida had gone.

"A shepherd—German shepherd, I guess. Peter claims it's an Alsatian shepherd, but I can't for the life of me figure out what the difference is. If there is a difference. Looks like a regular German shepherd to me."

"Have to ask someone who knows. Where did you pick him up?"

With a sense of relief, Jackie embarked on the tale of the dog's arrival. Mark was intrigued.

"A bullet? Poor guy. He must have rubbed someone the wrong way, all right. Are you going to keep him?"

"We'll see. I was worried that Peter would get too attached to him, and then have to say good-bye. He's a good dog, though, and he seems well trained. And after what happened here yesterday—" Jackie shivered.

The faculty lounge had emptied, except for the two of them. Mark led her over to a worn green-vinyl sofa. "Tell me what happened, Jackie. You seem all shook up."

"Of course I'm shook up, Mark. The man was just dead, there on the floor. It was terrible."

"And the police definitely think it was murder?"

She shrugged her shoulders, and her black curls shimmered. "Apparently he was poisoned. That's all I know," she lied. "I haven't really discussed it with anyone, except the lieutenant."

"Come on, Jackie. Aren't you curious?"

"I'm scared to death. And, frankly, Mark—in a situation like this, I think the safest course is to keep your curiosity under wraps."

"Hmm." Mark adjusted a carefully creased trouser leg and looked at his watch. "Nine-fifteen. I'd better get a move on. See you at noon?"

Jackie nodded, and Freeman departed.

There was still more than an hour before her first class. In spite of what she'd said to Mark Freeman, she really was curious—about Barger, and about the person who had murdered him. The murderer had come and gone at the Longacre Center without attracting attention. Of course the building had been deserted, or nearly; but Barger's office would be difficult to find if you didn't know your way around. Which left little doubt in Jackie's mind that the person was a member of the department, or at the very least a member of the university. A fellow teacher, or perhaps a student.

There were a handful of graduate students at the Longacre Center, all deeply engrossed in some aspect or other of the communications arts. Only one of them, Sylvie Thompson, had worked closely with Barger on her thesis, but as department chairman, the dead man had had a lot of influence over everyone's life.

The undergraduates were far more numerous, of course; but only a small percentage of those who browsed through the elective offerings at the Center became department majors. There might be fifteen or twenty majors, in the junior and senior classes.

Then there was the faculty. In addition to Jackie, Mark Freeman, David Surtees, and Merida Green, there were five full-time faculty members at the Longacre Center: Yelena Gruber, a temperamental beauty from Hungary who taught acting and directing; Jonathan Kersch, a retired theatrical producer who taught arts administration and business-related courses; Fred Jackson, a bearded bon vivant and cinematography instructor; Keith Monahan, a sober thirty-five-year-old who taught radio arts; and Marcus Baghorn, a sleek, fast-talking man of middle age whose specialty was advertising and marketing communications.

Only Fred Jackson, David Surtees, and Mark Freeman were members of the film department, but the other members of the Communications School certainly had known Barger well. Except for Surtees, they had all been at the

Center, in one connection or another, for ten years or more. And then, of course, there was Polly Merton.

Jackie mentally added the numbers. It came to nearly thirty people in close daily contact with Barger, one way or another. She felt she could rule out David Surtees; surely he wouldn't have opened the door to the editing room yesterday morning if he had stowed a body in there the night before.

On the other hand, there was the much-touted desire of all murderers to return to the scene of the crime. And if Surtees had left some kind of incriminating evidence, such as fingerprints on the body (was it possible to leave fingerprints on a body? she wondered)—well, then, his "discovery" of the dead man in Jackie's company would provide the perfect cover, an unchallengeable justification for footprints and fingerprints. Right down to fingerprints on Polly Merton's key, she reflected.

Which brought her thoughts back to Polly. Polly—as everyone knew—-was a by-the-book kind of departmental secretary. It was her thankless job to keep supplies on hand, to keep the photocopiers in good working order, to schedule meetings and send out all manner of notices, and to handle the chairman's correspondence to all department members and to the dean, the provost, and the trustees. Polly Merton was discreet and fastidious; she ruled with an iron fist in an iron glove. She had kept Barger at a safe distance, which must have taken some doing; for Polly was an attractive woman, if you could overlook her icy manner and the nunlike outfits that she wore. And Barger had managed to overlook more than that, in his career.

On the whole, thought Jackie, as she reviewed these personages in her mind, it was probably high time for a talk with Polly Merton.

Jackie entered the secretary's office from the hall, noting the yellow police tape that sealed off the door within that led to Barger's office. Polly was dressed appropriately for the day following the untimely death of the chairman. A long-sleeved blouse, perfectly white and perfectly pressed, hung loosely atop a dark skirt of worsted wool that drooped in monastic folds nearly to the floor. Her eyes—a hard blue—stared out at Jackie from behind no-nonsense steel-rimmed glasses; her long, very dark hair had been tied back in a bun that suggested the patience and virtue of a Jane Eyre.

Polly Merton was about Jackie's own age, but to Jackie she always seemed much older, thanks to her stiff-backed authority and her air of abstemious fortitude. Polly Merton ran a tight ship; you couldn't wipe your nose at the Longacre Center without a go-ahead from her.

After exchanging a few polite words of greeting, Jackie got to the point.

"I wanted to talk to you about those keys of yours, Polly," said Jackie, feeling rather as though she were challenging a she-bear in her den.

Polly looked at Jackie in surprise. "If you don't mind my saying so, I don't see what business any of it is of yours."

"Of course it's my business. It's everyone's business."

"I don't see it. Sorry."

"Polly—just tell me. Were your keys to the editing lab locked up?"

"They always are. You know that perfectly well."

"Then how—"

"The person who put Philip Barger's body in that room must have used Philip's key. He always carried it on his ring, and the police told me that his key ring was found with the body. No one came into this office that night, or used my keys."

"Ahh—" Jackie began, then caught herself. Maybe it would be better to keep her counsel about Barger's key, just for the moment, at least. "Well, if that person *hadn't* used Philip's key, is there another?"

Polly shook her head firmly. "No. And there never has been another."

"But what if someone had made a duplicate, somehow?"

"I would have known about it. Any unauthorized use of that room comes swiftly to my attention, Jackie. Which reminds me—what were you doing in there yesterday morning?" With an efficient gesture, she flipped the calendar to the previous day. "I told David Surtees the room was free—which it was. You weren't scheduled until tomorrow for that lab, and you didn't go through channels—"

"Oh." Jackie was momentarily stuck. She thought fast. "I just wanted to have a look around, check on all the equipment. You know. I'm a little bit rusty on teaching these lab sessions, after all. Since David was there and could let me in, without bothering anyone—I hope you don't mind?"

It was an awkward, fumbling kind of lie, but Polly Merton seemed to buy it.

"You really ought to check with me first, Jackie. We need to stick by the rules around here, you know. It's important for everyone's well-being. Especially now."

Jackie didn't feel much like being drawn into a discussion on departmental well-being, so she took her leave of Polly and headed down the hall to her own office and settled down to work on a pile of midterm papers. But she was deeply distracted and found it impossible to concentrate. What on earth had happened to the note that she had left for Polly? Barger had promised to put it on her desk, but surely Polly Merton would have mentioned it this morning if she'd received it. If only to admonish Jackie for not going through the proper channels.

And if the killer had found it, he (or she, Jackie mentally amended) would have known that the body would be discovered quickly, first thing in the morning. If that were the case, Jackie reasoned, there would be little point in moving the body—a risky proposition, even late at night in a deserted building.

No. It didn't wash, thought Jackie. The only reason to put Barger's body in the editing room would be to prevent its early discovery. Which meant that the killer, if somehow he had taken Polly Merton's keys from her locked drawer, did not see the note. But the note hadn't been found. Which meant that there had been yet another person present in the building on the night of the murder. Someone who had read the note? Or taken it, with a promise to give it to Polly?

Jackie glanced at the clock on her desk. Time for Film History 101.

As the class broke up and Jackie returned to her office, she was not at all surprised to find Lieutenant McGowan waiting for her.

"I have to rush to a meeting, Lieutenant," Jackie told him. "Can it wait?"

"Not really. Won't take a minute." He leaned up against Jackie's office door and gave her a smile, which she did her best to ignore. There was no question that the lieutenant was an attractive man, but Jackie was firmly determined to keep out of the way of attractive men for the time being. Her son needed a full-time mother, and romance just didn't fit the picture. Right now, anyway.

McGowan sensed her aloofness, and assumed a more businesslike expression. "There is a young woman in your class by the name of Danielle Sherman."

"Yes." Jackie tried to keep her expression noncommittal.

"We're going to have to question her. I just wanted to ask, before I meet with her, whether you might be able to give me any background. Off the record, of course."

Jackie shrugged her shoulders. "She's a good student. Bright, with a sharp eye for the visual elements. Rather quiet in class."

McGowan pulled a lopsided grin. "I think we both know that I'm not really after her intellectual credentials here."

Jackie thought a moment, then unlocked her office door and gestured McGowan in. "Have a seat, Lieutenant. I have five minutes."

"The word has reached us that Barger had quite a reputation among the students here," said McGowan, pulling up the visitor's chair and taking a seat.

"We discussed that last night." She tossed her lecture notes on the desk and rummaged in the top drawer for a notebook. "Didn't we?"

"We did. We didn't discuss names, however."

"No." Jackie stood her ground.

"I've learned that Danielle Sherman was having a relationship with Barger."

"Was she?"

"I believe so. I need to question her, Mrs. Walsh—and I was merely hoping that you could provide me with some insight before I proceed. Is she high-strung? Nervous? Confident? Self-assured?"

"Really, Lieutenant." Jackie was finding it difficult not to slip into the easy confidence this man offered. "I really don't think I'm the best judge of that. She seems fine in class, but what you're talking about—well, it's a different matter entirely. Some remarkably strong and confident women go to pieces in romantic relationships, and some airheaded bimboes are positively magisterial when it comes to a love affair. It's a toss-up, and it depends mostly on chemistry, in my view."

"Chemistry."

"Yeah, chemistry," replied Jackie evenly.

"Okay, then. She hasn't confided in you, or discussed this affair with you?"

"Lord, no. I'm a teacher, not a den mother, Lieutenant. And we all make it a rule not to stick our noses into Philip's little goings-on."

"Better that way, I suppose."

"People have got to look after themselves."

"I suppose so. Somebody was looking after himself—or herself—the other night, when Philip Barger was poisoned." He rose to go. "Thank you so much, Mrs. Walsh." He departed.

"Damn," said Jackie to herself. Then she gathered up her notebook and made a beeline for the faculty conference room.

The university's dean of faculty, B. Crowder Westfall, was a thin man with leathery skin, a tight-lipped smile, and a habit of making jokes that nobody understood. He was a classicist; and his references to the works of Livy and Juvenal and Aristophanes were, alas, lost on many of the faculty members and nearly all of the student body. B. Crowder Westfall had grown accustomed, over the course of thirty-two years as a professor and administrator, to the blank-eyed stares of professors and assistant professors and students outside of his own department. Their ignorance of the great works of western culture tugged at his heartstrings and made him sad, but he had learned to live with his dismay.

At the noon meeting in the Longacre Center, B. Crowder Westfall was addressing the assembled members of the communications faculty. As was his custom in making speeches, he drew on the methods, and indeed the words, of the great orators of antiquity. In his address to the department, he alluded generously to everyone's grief at the passing of so esteemed a colleague, nicely skirting over the brutal manner of that passing, and detouring altogether, for the moment, around the guilt or innocence of his audience members. He roused the department to momentary harmony and fellow feeling, stirring in their breasts a common sense of purpose that they had not felt since the old coffee percolator in the lounge had given out. Nothing of a practical nature was accomplished, however, beyond the appointment of Merida Green as chairwoman pro tem of the film department. This arrangement seemed to satisfy everyone.

With this duty accomplished, Westfall drew Jackie aside.

"Mrs. Walsh, please allow me to extend my deepest sympathies to you. I am sure that your experiences of yesterday

were difficult indeed; but I have every expectation that you
will, in time, overcome the ill effects, if any, of such a
shock."

"Thank you very much, Dr. Westfall," Jackie replied
politely. She was a little better versed in the classics than
some of her colleagues, and she had a genuine fondness
for the old man, who had taught her ancient Greek. "It
really *was* a shock, of course; but I'm glad you've been
so quick to help us overcome any administrative hurdles
that we might have faced."

"Yes, well, ahem." He took Jackie by the arm and guided
her gently down the corridor toward her office. "If we might
have a word or two in private?"

Jackie obliged, wondering what on earth the old man
could want to discuss with her.

"The university is of course much distressed by the loss
of so distinguished a man," Westfall said with a twinkle in
his eye as he took a seat. "And I don't mean to be indeco-
rous, or unseemly, in rushing forward with certain rather
mundane matters. I hope you will understand, though, that
however deep our grief we must press ahead. Press right
ahead."

"Yes, I understand, Dr. Westfall."

"Good. Well—I want to make it clear that I speak for the
president as well as for myself, Mrs. Walsh, in making a
request of you."

"I'll be only too happy to help, in whatever way I can,
sir," she replied, feeling that an ominous request was coming. It was very like Henry Obermaier, the university's
president, to make demands on the faculty through a hapless
third party like Westfall.

"Good. I knew you would. Now—the thing is, this Kestrel project is fairly well advanced, I understand; and the
significance of such an undertaking has not been lost on
the, er, ahem, the board of trustees."

"No," agreed Jackie, comprehension beginning to dawn.
There was money at stake for the university. She waited.

"So. We have discussed the need to follow through on this project—did you know that Stuart Goodwillie is interested in it?"

"I knew that his money was behind it. At least, that was the rumor going around."

"Yes, indeed. Well, it's not a rumor, not at all. Needless to say, the trustees are most interested in pursuing *his* interest, if you follow me."

"I'm not certain I do."

"He apparently considers the work of Graham Grosset—in particular, the Kestrel books—to be the finest writing of the twentieth century. And as an alumnus of Rodgers, he would very much like to secure for the university the acclaim that such a project will bring. So much so that he has even spoken of endowing a new building for the Longacre Center, in recognition of our having helped bring these books to the screen."

"Wow!" remarked Jackie.

Stuart Goodwillie was a very rich man—the richest in Palmer, by a long stretch. He had started out life as a research chemist, a quirky genius, and he had built up his fortune through a series of happy accidents in his research on polymer bonding. He held patents on materials with a thousand and one uses, which had been deployed in every industry from toy manufacture to nuclear armaments.

But as everyone in Palmer knew, Goodwillie had a passion for the movies. Several times, as a younger man, he had attempted to produce films, but each experiment had fallen flat. Just last year, however, he had formed a new production company, and he was determined to have one great film to his credit before he died. Westfall explained to Jackie that through a complicated series of trusts and contracts, Goodwillie had tied up the production company with a promised endowment to the university. And because Goodwillie was well advanced in years, the trustees quite naturally wanted to keep on the best of terms with their eccentric billionaire.

"That endowment," Westfall was saying, "would be con-
tingent upon our being able to complete the project. Which
has now, unfortunately, come to a hiatus. And this, my good
Mrs. Walsh, is where you come in."

Jackie swallowed. This was beginning to sound like a
great deal of responsibility. "I see."

"Yes. We would very much appreciate it, the president
and I, if you could do a little bit of the legwork here among
Professor Barger's papers. We need, first and foremost, to
see just how far along he was with the drama—the, er,
screenplay, I believe it is called."

"Right. The screenplay." Jackie breathed a sigh of relief.
This would be easy, given Polly Merton's propensity for
tidiness. She probably had everything neatly docketed and
filed, awaiting Barger's revisions and comments. "I will get
on that right away, Dr. Westfall," she said.

"Very good. Thank you so very much." He stopped at
the doorway and remarked, "I think it might be well for
you to talk to our esteemed visiting colleague, as well. Just
touch base, you know. Make sure everything can proceed
apace."

"Certainly," said Jackie, pleased at the prospect of a
tête-à-tête with Graham Grosset. "No problem."

CHAPTER 5

At five o'clock in the afternoon, Cosmo Gordon sat at his gray metal desk, glaring into the unsightly remains of a cup of coffee. Before him were the preliminary findings on the death of Philip Barger, Ph.D. The lab had found that Barger had ingested a large quantity of hydrocyanic acid—enough to cause an almost immediate collapse. Death had been swift, Gordon reflected. At least Barger's killer had done him a kindness there, sparing him the infinitely long moments of violent illness that accompanied smaller doses of the poison.

The case was a problem, no doubt about it. Palmer had its share of homicides, of course; but chiefly they were the shoot-and-run sort that accompanied robbery and other violent activities. The sort of thing, in all likelihood, that had happened to Matt Dugan. Or else the homicides were the outgrowth of domestic unhappiness. Gordon had seen a great number of cases in which husband had pitted himself against wife, or son against parent. Those were more understandable, in their way.

Gordon reached for the phone and dialed Lieutenant McGowan. The two men were good friends; the medical examiner had helped McGowan on many of his cases, as he climbed the ranks in the Palmer police.

"Mike? Gordon here. No doubt about it: cause of death was poisoning by hydrocyanic acid. Quite a large dose."

McGowan jotted down the details. "Thanks, Cosmo. If you're finished there, how about a beer? The Juniper, fifteen minutes?"

The Juniper Tavern was a comfortable, smoky, friendly kind of place, a favorite haunt of both the working classes and the nearby university types—thanks to the cook's great skill with hamburgers and the sophisticated assortment of beers on tap, both of which were great levelers in the stratified arena of university life. The old-fashioned bar was a good thirty feet long, and made of solid mahogany; on the far side of it was an equally long mirrored mahogany cabinet dating from the turn of the century. The sinks at each end were marble, with brass fittings; and the tap handles were porcelain. All in all, a wonderful place for a policeman, or anyone, at the end of a long working day.

"Thanks for coming," said McGowan as they settled onto their bar stools. "What will you have?"

"English."

"Two English, Milt," said McGowan, tossing a ten-dollar bill on the bar. He sighed. "It's a poser, Cosmo."

"You have a suspect yet?" asked the older man as their frosty pints arrived.

"Cheers. No."

"What about the people who found the body?"

"I'm working on them first, of course. One of them's brand-new to the Longacre Center—a guy called Surtees. Only been there since September, and I think he's pretty much on the up-and-up. The other one is a woman, divorced, who used to teach here before she was married. She came back in September, without her husband."

"Women's-Lib type? Stringy hair and a chip on her shoulder?"

McGowan shook his head firmly. "You mean like Bonnie Greenstein?" Bonnie Greenstein was a campus fixture; in the late sixties, she had cut a swath through the political life at Rodgers, putting up placards and howling at her fellow students through a megaphone. Now well past forty, she had apparently never been able to make another career for herself; so she persisted in organizing caucuses and bellowing through her megaphone whenever the opportunity arose. Over her many years of tireless work, she had become well known to the Palmer police. "No. Jackie Walsh is a bright, nice lady, Cosmo."

"Can she give you anything?"

"Just problems," McGowan said with a wry grin. He then proceeded to relate the tale of the key, and the rescheduled editing lab. "So I figured somebody must have had a key. A duplicate."

"That's easy, then. Just track the cutter."

McGowan shook his head. "Nope. The door's got a Hinsch lock, and I can't find a locksmith in the city who cut a spare. They have to keep records if they make a Hinsch duplicate, because of the insurance. And I've had three officers on it today. Turned up nothing."

"Not good for your nice lady who says she had the key, Mike."

"I know. But she's clean—I'd swear to it."

"Any history between her and Barger?"

"She says not. I believe her. Besides—she's got a kid, a boy about ten or so. I can't picture her filling up Barger's liqueur bottle with poison and then going home to help the kid with his arithmetic."

"Maybe you have a point. But it sounds like you've got a thing for this lady, Mike. Watch your step."

"Don't I know it," replied McGowan, signaling to the bartender for another round.

They drank their beer in silence for a time. Finally Gordon spoke again. "You say the other key was in the secretary's drawer. Locked up. Would she be ready to swear to that?"

"Yup." McGowan took a large swallow. "The secretary's name is Polly Merton. Looks like a nun or something—dresses in long black skirts, no makeup, hair tied in a knot."

"Repressed? Have a thing for Barger?"

"Yes and no. Definitely one of those sanctimonious types, with a thing about being organized. Like she's afraid it'll all spin out of control if she takes her eye off it for a minute."

"Hmm."

"But I would lay odds of a hundred to one against her having a thing with Barger. Too much of a schoolmistress. An affair with her boss would break the rules. So would murder."

"That's not evidence," Gordon pointed out amiably. "That's conjecture. And if you find a case against her, then the state can easily come up with an expert to break down that logic."

"Yeah." McGowan sat thoughtfully for a moment. "The guy had quite a reputation on campus, though."

"Oh? Important, you mean?"

"I mean getting involved with his students, one after another."

"Ah," said Gordon. "I'll bet there's something there. Poison—they always say it's a woman's weapon, don't they, Mike?"

"Sure do."

"So your next step—"

"Talk to all the broken hearts at Rodgers University. Not a problem."

Gordon chuckled. "Just make sure you don't break any hearts yourself along the way, Mike."

Cosmo Gordon headed home; and after a solitary burger at the Juniper Tavern, Michael McGowan returned to his office to read through the reports on Philip Barger. The case was already coming in for plenty of press coverage; and when it heated up, McGowan knew that the Palmer police were likely to take it on the chin, unless they could solve the murder quickly. A juicy case like this was a policeman's nightmare.

For all of his philandering, Philip Barger had led a rather friendless and solitary existence. The police reports were full of the details of the affairs with which Barger had regularly enlivened his evenings, but these relationships had been short and probably rather one-sided.

A female police officer had interviewed three of the young women with whom Barger had spent time in the last few years and none of them admitted to bearing a grudge. Danielle Sherman, the most recent of Barger's young targets, would be most likely to have strong feelings for him, but in her interview she had come across as levelheaded, and harboring no illusions as to the permanence of the relationship. In fact, she had been disturbingly pragmatic about it, and the transcript shattered McGowan's image of the tenderhearted young student dazzled by the brilliant and handsome professor.

Mary Richmond, on the other hand, sounded as though she might nurse a grudge. McGowan flipped through the transcript of her interview. Barger had thrown Richmond over last spring, shortly before the conclusion of the term. The young woman's grades had been poor; Richmond described her sleepless nights and her inability to concentrate at the most critical time in the semester. According to Officer Warner, the young woman had considered bringing a lawsuit against Barger, but had never done so, contenting herself with sending a barrage of threatening letters.

This looked much better, thought McGowan. He noted down Richmond's address, and set out to talk to her.

Peter Walsh, after lengthy conferences upon the subject with his friend Isaac Cook, had finally decided on a name for the dog. Jake.

"It's gotta sound kind of cool," Isaac had counseled, "but you gotta remember that it should be easy to pronounce. Short, with a lot of hard sounds in it. That's real important when you're training him."

"Yeah," agreed Peter. It was five-thirty in the afternoon, and although the evening air had a chill, and the sun was ready to set, the boys were in the small backyard at Peter's house, attempting to teach Jake to fetch a tennis ball. Jake, by nature and breeding disinclined to fetch, was nonetheless doing his best to be part of whatever game it was that his new small friend wanted to play. He cooperated, but in a dignified and measured way, without any of the giddy eagerness of the true retriever.

"So if the name's got a lot of hissy sounds, or mumbly sounds, the dog can't hear it right," Isaac went on. "I mean, you *could* name him Hero, but when you called him, you'd have to say 'Here, Hero,' and that sounds sort of dumb. He might not even get it."

"Hmm." Peter mulled this over, while Isaac expounded more fully. Isaac's own dogs were called Stella, Jojo, and Chopsticks; Peter mentally rehearsed their names, wondering if they really had the requisite bite or zing.

"I know a girl who calls her dog Cindy," Isaac was saying. "What a dumb dog. But it isn't the dog's fault. She can't ever tell if they're saying Cindy, or cinder block or sand or anything."

"Really dumb," Peter agreed.

"Plus, Jake's kind of an old dog, and you don't know what his name was before. So it's good to have a name that sticks out, kind of."

"Yeah," concurred Peter, once more throwing the tennis ball against the far wall. Jake—as he was to be known— trotted dutifully after the ball, with an air of forbearance and goodwill upon his handsome face.

"Let's see if he can do any tricks," advised Isaac. "Find out what he already knows."

Jake returned to the boys with the ball, and for several minutes he obliged the boys by sitting, lying down, and shaking with his good paw.

"He's been trained," Peter pointed out at last. "He can do all the basic stuff."

"Yeah. It doesn't look like his leg bothers him anymore," Isaac opined. "Did you believe that vet when he said it was a bullet wound?"

"He said he wasn't *sure,*" Peter clarified. "But by the shape of it, or whatever, he thought so." He threw the tennis ball.

"A rifle, maybe." Isaac looked carefully at Jake, sizing him up. "He doesn't look like a real fighter."

"He's hurt." Peter didn't want to hear criticism. "Look." He snapped his fingers, and Jake dropped the ball and came to him. Peter gingerly lifted the dog's paw. "The bandage covers it, mostly. But it's bad. *Really* bad. He lost a lot of blood, and he might have died. I think it must have been a fight."

Jake struggled out of Peter's grasp and sat down, holding his head high, and opening his mouth wide to pant contentedly. "See," Peter went on, "he gets tired kind of easy."

"Maybe because he's old," suggested Isaac.

"Maybe." Peter had been forced to admit to himself, last night before he fell asleep, that Hero—or Jake, as he now was called—*was* kind of old. Nothing that anybody could do about that. Peter would just have to work around it, keep the exercise regular but not too much. Make sure he got plenty of fresh air and good food. With any luck, the owners would never turn up.

"My mom says what's the difference between an Alsatian and a German shepherd," Peter said.

"There's a *big* difference," asserted Isaac. "First of all, Alsatians are easier to train. You can tell he's an Alsatian because he's been trained so well. Plus, Alsatians are bigger. Look at how big his head is. He's a big guy."

Peter agreed. He took a Magic Marker from the pocket of his jeans and stood up to measure Jake's head, marking the length (from the top of the head to the tip of the nose) on his arm. Then he measured the dog's head from side to side, carefully adding two more dots to his arm. Finally, he measured the distance between the tips of Jake's ears.

"I heard somewhere that you can tell how smart a dog is by how far it is from one ear to the other," said Peter. "Let's get a ruler. I think this is about six inches." He held up his arm.

"No, you can't," retorted Isaac, disdainful. "No way. The way you tell how smart a dog is, is by how well he can do tricks. Jake does pretty good tricks, for an old dog. He's pretty smart."

"Yeah," said Peter, pride in his voice. "He's really smart."

"Peter!" called Jackie from within. "Ask Isaac to call his mother if he wants to stay for dinner."

"Do you?" Peter looked at his friend. "Hot dogs, I think."

"Sure."

So Isaac Cook stayed to supper—hot dogs and french fries, with no hint of a green vegetable. Tonight, they were celebrating Jake's new name.

Over supper (after the dimensions of Jake's head had been carefully measured and recorded), Isaac provided Jackie and Peter with an earful of intimate knowledge of dogs and their ways. Jackie—who had had dogs aplenty when she was growing up—didn't bother to contradict Isaac on his more farfetched inventions. Isaac's dogs were all exceedingly well mannered, and where dogs were concerned that was more than half the battle, Jackie thought. Jake was also well mannered, and whatever standoffishness there had once been in his demeanor had disappeared. During dinner, he lay contentedly under the kitchen table, which was clearly his spot. He had taken to their family like a duck to water, she thought.

After supper, Jackie and Peter and Jake walked Isaac home, through the quiet streets that fronted the university. Isaac's mother was a teacher in the fine arts school; his father a specialist in Spanish and Portuguese literature. In the few short months since the boys had become friends, Jackie had grown to like the Cooks very much.

As they walked homeward again, Jake at their side, Jackie began to feel that all was indeed right with the world. She forgot, momentarily, the terrible events at the Longacre Center; and she was content in the company of her small boy and his beautiful new dog.

CHAPTER 6

On the following morning, Jackie Walsh was locked once more in a pointless debate with Polly Merton. Jackie was accustomed to it; no matter what the topic under discussion, Polly Merton had a way of making the subject both grander and more trivial than it really was. If you wanted to use the conference room, for example, Polly would want to know what your meeting concerned, and if you planned to use pencils and paper, and in general find a way to make your ideas sound like a ludicrous waste of the university's resources. If you backed down, tired of the struggle, and decided to hold the meeting in your own office, Polly was right there, accusing you of not being serious about your work. With Polly, it was always a lose-lose proposition for the faculty members.

But Jackie, in her naive or hopeful way, had thought that the matter of the Kestrel books would somehow be simpler. It was, after all, a straightforward thing that Westfall had asked: Jackie only needed to examine the screenplay for the Kestrel books, and assess the progress of the project.

"I don't even need to *see* the original, Polly, if you have a copy," Jackie said, her voice taking on an edge of impatience. "Even a disk from your computer will do just fine."

"You haven't explained why you need any of those materials," Polly asserted. She was dressed this morning in something that looked like a cross between riding clothes and an undertaker's suit. She looked with disdain at Jackie's short purple skirt and chartreuse overblouse. "Until I have instructions from the executor of Professor Barger's estate, my hands are tied."

"Polly, I am acting as a result of a direct request of the president and the trustees."

"They haven't spoken to me."

"No—no, Polly, they spoke to *me,* through Dr. Westfall. But now you may consider that they are speaking to you. Through me. Through Dr. Westfall. If you like, I can have him call you, or have the president call you directly, with their request. But wouldn't it be far simpler just to trust me?"

"I don't like it, not at all." But Polly had evidently considered that a call from the president might contain more than just an authorization for Jackie to see Barger's files, for she rose and withdrew a key from her drawer. "Follow me."

She opened the door of a small accessory closet, where the department's precious supplies of mimeograph forms, copier paper, and other office goodies were kept. Polly Merton maintained the strictest security over the little room and its contents, as Jackie well knew; and anyone needing supplies was constrained to wait upon Polly Merton's pleasure. Which did not manifest itself often.

Giving Jackie a warning glare, Polly unlocked a small, two-drawer file and stooped to look through the top rank of manila folders.

"Dr. Barger kept a few things in here," she said. "He was very particular about keeping them under lock and key." Jackie peered over Polly's shoulder as she rummaged. When she reached the end, she started at the beginning again. Then she opened the bottom drawer, which was empty, except for two videocassettes lying forlornly at the bottom.

Then she opened another cabinet and conducted a similar search, with no result.

"He must have put them somewhere else," Jackie suggested. "Maybe in his office."

Polly slammed the drawer shut and turned on Jackie. "You were here, before. You took them."

"No, honestly—no. I haven't been near Barger's files."

Polly stalked out of the room, and Jackie followed, feeling ridiculous. "Polly, could we just have a look at that other file cabinet?"

"There's nothing of Dr. Barger's in my files," sniffed Polly. "I keep only the department files."

"All right. Well, thanks for trying. I'm sure the materials will surface." They had returned to Polly's office, and Jackie looked at the door that led into Barger's room. It was still sealed with yellow police tape. "Maybe when the police unseal that room," she said.

Jackie was determined to keep her promise to B. Crowder Westfall. She realized that she had been very lucky to secure her job; and although she was utterly without ambition of the administrative sort—she had no longing at all for power within the department—she did very much want to do well and to be able to expand her curriculum over the next few years. It wouldn't do to disappoint the president and the trustees. After a few moments of reflection, she reached for the telephone book. Then she dialed the Palmer police.

Lieutenant Michael McGowan was pleased to hear from her—there was little doubt about that. Jackie took advantage.

"What can I do for you, Mrs. Walsh?"

"Well, Lieutenant, I am hoping that you might be able to let me into Philip's office. It's still all sealed up."

"It is indeed. We haven't solved the crime yet, in case you hadn't heard."

"Oh! I didn't mean to sound critical, Lieutenant. It's just that we're looking for something, and I thought perhaps it was in there. That's all."

"What are you looking for?"

"Some papers that he was working on. You remember that we discussed the Kestrel project."

McGowan did remember. Jackie explained briefly about Westfall's request, and he said that he would see what he could do.

"I think I'd prefer to keep everyone out of there, for the time being. You understand, I'm sure, that even though the trail grows cold, when we catch our murderer we don't want to run the risk of having tainted the evidence."

"No, of course not," said Jackie. He promised to send someone over at lunchtime. She thanked him and made a mad dash for her classroom.

After class, she walked to the faculty lounge, where she discovered Lieutenant McGowan, who had made himself at home. He greeted her with a friendly air, dangling a ring of keys before her.

"I've come to help you in your search," he said with a smile.

Uh-oh, thought Jackie. "Thanks very much, Lieutenant." She allowed him to lead the way to Barger's office, and together they removed the yellow tape that sealed the door.

"Aren't you worried about tainting the evidence?" she asked him as he removed the last strip of tape.

"Nope. I've got protection." He patted his pocket and opened the door.

Jackie looked about. Everything was just the same, but irretrievably altered. It was strange how death did that to a place. She thought briefly of the little room on the third floor that had been her father's office. He was a writer, and in his little aerie he had penned a dozen or more movie scripts (only three ever made it to production), hundreds of movie reviews for magazines and newspapers, and several dozen episodes of his pet project, *Long Arm of the Law,* a television show that had failed to beat out *Highway Patrol,* and had died a quiet death. After her father died, the room had changed; and Jackie knew then as now that the change had been real; it was not just her imagination telling her so.

Then as now, the change was palpable.

McGowan gave her a few moments. Then he said quietly, "It always feels strange, being in a place like this."

She gave him a smile and rolled up her sleeves, to prove that she was equal to the task.

"Where would these papers be?" McGowan asked, withdrawing a small tape recorder from his pocket. "Protection," he added with a wink.

"Where? Got me. Probably in the desk."

They made their way around the other side of Barger's huge teak desk and McGowan began to pull open the drawers, speaking softly into the tape recorder as he did so.

"Top right desk drawer. Envelopes. Roll of stamps. Small hand-held calculator. Pencils, pens." He shut the drawer and moved on to the next.

The search of the desk was followed by a quick look through the famous credenza, which held nothing but liquor, a variety of glasses, and, in a concealed compartment, a stack of girlie magazines and a row of videotapes. There was a gap in the rank of bottles where the almond liqueur had stood; it gave Jackie the shivers.

"Nope. Not here, Mrs. Walsh. Sorry." McGowan lifted a brow. "You're certain that these papers were in the dead man's possession?"

Jackie nodded. "He told me—that night, he said he would be staying late, working on the script. It was right on his desk."

"You're sure that's what you saw there?"

"Pretty sure. It was definitely a script; and I can't imagine that Barger was working on anything else. He wasn't what you might call industrious." She grinned.

"I see." McGowan scratched his head. "The secretary?"

Jackie shook her head firmly. "We looked. Barger's papers were all kept in a little storeroom on the other side of Polly's office. She went through all of the things in there this morning."

"*She* did?"

"While I watched."

"Right. Wish I'd known about those files. I should have been there."

"We didn't take anything out. And the filing cabinets are locked. So your evidence is intact, Lieutenant."

"Good. Along with it, my professional self-esteem." He glanced at his watch. "How about a little lunch?"

Jackie thought this a fine idea. "Let me just get something from my office. Then I'll take you to the canteen, if you can bear three-day-old egg salad."

"Only three days? A policeman's dream."

Jackie grabbed her coat, purse, and a manila envelope from her office, and they were on their way.

The campus was quiet. Midterm examinations would start on Monday, and the main quadrangle, shaded by large old sycamores and surrounded on three sides by imposing neo-Gothic buildings, was comparatively deserted. They made their way through the late-fall sunshine toward the Sturbinger Building, a large, squat, red-brick structure that was mercifully hidden from view behind the graceful facade of Wescott Hall. As they walked, Jackie told McGowan a little bit about the buildings and the school; and although the police lieutenant was well acquainted with the layout and history of Rodgers University, he didn't interrupt. He enjoyed her cheerful prattling.

"My son and I found a dog," she said at last as they reached the building and made their way to the cafeteria within.

"Yes, I know," McGowan replied as they joined the line for lunch. "Damn. I forgot to put that sign up at the precinct house." He shot Jackie a regretful look as he handed her a tray.

She laughed. "You can have one of our new, improved signs, Lieutenant, and I'll keep your failed promise a secret from Peter." They piled their trays high with sandwiches, yogurt, potato chips, and soft drinks, and found a table in a quiet corner. McGowan noted that Jackie seemed to have a healthy appetite, despite the evident strain of searching Barger's office. He approved of hardy women.

Jackie opened her manila envelope and produced a flier. "We took a Polaroid of Jake last night, and I enlarged it at the copy shop." She handed the flier over. "Handsome, isn't he?"

"A very good-looking animal," McGowan agreed. "What does he do, while you're at work all day?"

"He stays in our backyard—not much more than a patch of dirt, really. But he likes it. At night he comes in."

"Ah," remarked McGowan. "Fallen for him, I see. Well. This one will go up on the wall. I promise."

"Thanks." Jackie brushed a dark lock off her forehead and took a thoughtful bite of her egg-salad sandwich. "I'm of two minds about that dog," she said. "He doesn't seem to care that we're not his real family, which is kind of unnerving. Makes you wonder if he's loyal, or just an opportunist. I mean, did he throw his owners over?" She told McGowan the entire story of Jake's appearance at their kitchen door and the trip to the vet.

"A bullet wound?" McGowan asked. "That's strange."

"I thought so too," Jackie agreed. "At first I was reluctant to take him on, because I thought he might be one of those wild dogs that you hear about. But he seems very good-natured and amazingly well trained. Obviously, he used to have a home somewhere. And then—after what happened—I decided it might be a good idea to keep him around, for as long as he wants to stay. Comforting."

"I would think so," McGowan replied firmly. He was a little old-fashioned, and he wasn't sure he liked the idea of Jackie and her young son living alone in that old renovated building. But it was no business of his, he admonished himself. "Dogs are a good thing to have."

"I agree. My former husband was allergic to them— to dogs, cats, anything with fur." Jackie colored as she mentioned Cooper, conscious of a curious urge to confide in McGowan. She brushed the impulse aside. "About the case," she said firmly. "We might as well get on with it. Shoot."

" 'Shoot'?"

"Yes. Don't you want to question me further? That is why you wanted to have lunch, isn't it?"

McGowan looked steadily at her. "No."

"Oh."

"But—since you offered—"

"Go ahead," invited Jackie, relieved and disappointed at once. "Shoot."

McGowan smiled at her. "You've told me everything I need to know."

"Oh!" Jackie ate her sandwich in silence for a few moments. "Well, then. Have you got a key to Barger's house?"

"Sure. On his key ring."

"So you can take me over there, after we finish our lunch, and we can continue our search for the Kestrel screenplay. All right?"

"All right," agreed McGowan, grateful that this was all in the line of duty. He would hate to have to explain today's outing to the captain. McGowan's superior officer could be a real bear about procedure, when he chose.

Philip Barger's house, like his office, was a monument to the self-congratulatory, sybaritic life-style that he had embodied. The outside gave little hint of his taste (or lack thereof); his was one in a neat rank of late nineteenth-century rowhouses in a block known familiarly as Faculty Lane. The little street was really not more than a mews, separated from the main thoroughfares of Walnut and Chestnut streets by iron gratings at each end.

This part of the university community was inhabited mostly by professors and university administrators, and Faculty Lane was by far the nicest block of all. The university's president occupied the largest residence on the block—a grand edifice made up of two beautiful houses that had been knocked together into one. Barger's house was at the far end, near Chestnut Street.

McGowan led the way up the marble stairs and unlocked the door. "I've only had time for a quick look around in here," he commented, "but some of our people have been over it carefully. I gather it's kind of unusual. I don't know if you're going to like what you see."

"Don't worry about my feminine feelings," replied Jackie with a laugh. "I think I may know what to expect."

Barger had really let himself go in decorating the place. Most of the furniture was of leather—sleek skins that conveyed a sense, somehow, of live animal passions. There were plenty of glass-and-chrome tables, and lamps with red light bulbs hidden by black shades. A library or den toward the back of the house had been transformed into a kind of grotesque, ersatz jungle, with *faux* leopard-skin rugs, sofas of butter-soft leather, an assortment of tropical plants (all in desperate need of water), and a bar with mirrors and an abundance of bottles. One wall was almost entirely taken up by a huge zebra skin; Jackie smirked at this, wondering if Barger had known that the zebra is an animal of wide-open grasslands. The other walls were adorned with hugely enlarged color photographs of the dead man: steering a sailboat on some body of blue water, reclining on a beach with a bikini-clad young woman, hitting a tennis ball on a tennis court somewhere. The room was pathetic, and it made Jackie feel queasy.

Jackie and McGowan made quick work of the ground floor. The house was nearly devoid of any of the familiar trappings of scholarship; there were only one or two bookcases, and these contained large-format coffee-table books, by and large. There was no evidence that the man could actually read, thought Jackie in amazement.

The upstairs contained more of the same. The guest bedrooms were sparsely furnished, but even so the aura of male mischief pervaded: the closets held a variety of negligees, slippers, and other ladylike nightwear. The master

bedroom was predictably fitted out with an ultra-large bed
and mirrors everywhere. A huge oak wardrobe contained
more clothes than Jackie had ever seen accumulated in
one place—except, perhaps, in the "shirt scene" in the
movie version of *The Great Gatsby*. Or its modern-day
equivalent in *American Gigolo*. And on the walls were more
photographs of Barger—playing golf, sipping champagne,
and otherwise in hot pursuit of the ultimate good time.

Jackie was quiet as they made their search. The house
depressed her, making her realize how difficult life must
have been for Celestine Barger before she made her great
escape. By comparison, the unhappiness that Jackie had felt
during the years while her own marriage failed seemed like
child's play. Cooper had been, at least, a gentleman in the
way he conducted his affair. And he had displayed very
good taste in having only one mistress.

The search took less than forty-five minutes. When every
drawer and closet had been opened, and the contents of
all the boxes in the third-floor storage rooms had been
examined, Jackie and Lieutenant McGowan beat a hasty
retreat.

"Whew!" Jackie exclaimed as McGowan locked the front
door behind them, and they stepped out once more into the
fresh fall air. "I always knew that man was bad news.
Creepy. Like Richard Crenna in *Wait Until Dark*."

"Well—at least he wasn't a murderer stalking a blind
woman," replied McGowan. "I've seen worse—but not in
a setting like this, if you know what I mean."

"I do," Jackie responded.

McGowan took his leave of her, but not before promis-
ing, once more, to post Jake's photo at the office. "Missing
persons may have something to tell us too. It could be that
it's the owner who's lost, and not the dog," he told Jackie,
with a broad grin.

As she returned to the Longacre Center, Jackie nearly
collided with Danielle Sherman, who was rushing hurriedly
out through the lobby exit.

"Oh! Hi," said Danielle, her face flushed.

"Hi, Danielle. How are you?"

"Fine, thanks. Fine," replied the young woman, swallowing hard and clutching at her heavy bookbag. "I was just upstairs in the library, watching *The Battleship Potemkin.*" She stared at Jackie. "For my paper. For your class."

"Danielle—is everything okay?"

"Of course." Danielle took a step back into the building.

"Um, Danielle—do you have a second?"

"Sure."

"Good. Listen," said Jackie, taking her elbow and beginning to lead her farther indoors. "I'm glad I ran into you. I thought maybe we ought to have a talk."

"A talk." Danielle stared dumbly at Jackie. "Okay. What about?"

"Well, for starters, about Philip."

The blood drained from Danielle's skinny, perfectly made-up face. She brushed back a dark curl from her forehead. "I'd rather not, if you don't mind."

"I can understand that this situation must be difficult for you," pursued Jackie. "But you see, I need your help."

"*My* help?"

"Yes." They had reached a group of leather settees that formed a seating area just outside the doors to the Center's small, informal theater. The building was very quiet. Jackie sat down, and Danielle Sherman followed suit, her reluctance evident. "It's politics, really—but the trustees very much wish to go ahead with the filming of *Kestrel.* Unfortunately, nobody seems to know where Philip put the script that he wrote. And I thought, under the circumstances, that you might have some kind of idea?"

Danielle Sherman shook her head firmly. "No. No idea."

"You did know he was working on it?"

"Well, yeah. I mean, it was a big topic of conversation. In general, I mean—in class. They're *great* books."

"Did Philip ever talk to you about the screenplay?"

"Nope."

"Or about how the deal was structured, or what he thought of Graham Grosset, or what Grosset thought of him?"

"Nope."

Good Lord, thought Jackie. *What* had *they talked about?* "And you didn't know, did you, that Philip would be there by himself that night, working on it?"

"Look, Mrs. Walsh—"

"Call me Jackie."

"Okay, I will. Look. Philip and I had an affair. Big deal. It was over, in fact, before he—before then. I told him I didn't want to see him anymore. It was getting boring."

"Hardly surprising, if he wouldn't talk to you about the most interesting thing in his life."

"What we talked about is *our* business. Was our business."

"Right. Sorry."

"Look, I have to go. I'll see you in class. But please— don't ask me any more questions. And don't go telling people about me and Philip. It might ruin things for me."

"Sure," replied Jackie with little conviction. She was fairly sure that Danielle Sherman was well on the way to ruining things for herself.

Jackie made her way home, still reveling in the urban delight of walking from place to place. Jackie and Peter lived between the campus and the Palmer Museum of Fine Arts, in a reclaimed no-man's-land that had once been given over to light industry. Fifteen years ago, when Jackie had first begun her teaching career, the neighborhood had been considered seedy; the cobblers and textile workers who had once sweated in these buildings were long gone, and no one would have dreamed of living there. But this part of Palmer, like similar areas in a hundred cities across the United States, had experienced a renaissance. First had come the adventurous young families; and then the real-estate speculators. By the time Jackie and Peter moved in to their loft on Isabella Lane, the neighborhood had become downright upright.

Jackie lost herself in thought as she walked. She was more puzzled than ever that Barger had managed to get the rights to the Kestrel books.

The story that Graham Grosset told in his novels—of genius obsessed with the need for revenge—was almost prim, in a way. Certainly there was nothing lascivious about it. The central character in the trilogy was a Renaissance architect who blames the Catholic Church in general, and the Pope in particular, for the death of his only son. He sets out on a course of evil, hoping to find salvation for his child's soul through a misguided attempt at murder. The books were a fabulous mixture of suspense and theology, art history and passion, love and murder. Their author was a man of great erudition—the Hodgman Prize, which Grosset had received for the trilogy, was an extremely high honor.

How could Graham Grosset possibly have put his greatest work in the hands of a nobody like Philip Barger? Now that she had seen the pitiful trappings of the man's life, Jackie was more intrigued than ever.

CHAPTER 7

When Jackie returned to the department after her exploratory mission to Barger's house, her mail slot was brimming with pink telephone-message slips. She flipped through them quickly. Three calls had come from Dr. Westfall's office, two from the office of the president, one from Jason Huckle, and two from her ex-husband. Jackie rolled her eyes and picked up the one from Jason Huckle. Who on earth was Jason Huckle? Of course—the dog's doctor. That was surely the most interesting of the bunch. Perhaps he had a lead on Jake's owners, she thought with a sinking feeling. She headed for her office and dialed the number.

"Hi, Dr. Huckle," she said. "This is Jackie Walsh, returning your call."

"Ah, yes. Ms. Walsh. Thank you for calling. I just wanted to let you know that I have back the results of a few tests I ran on that dog. Do you still have him?"

"Oh, yes. Peter and I have even given him a name." Test results. Jackie's heart began to race. What if Jake had some terrible disease? Had she exposed Peter to the dangers of a violent, unpredictable, possibly rabid animal? Would Jake have to be put down?

"Good. Nothing makes a dog happier than having a name," replied Huckle. Jackie breathed more easily. Apparently Jake wasn't a dangerous beast. "Well, then. I took some X rays of that fracture, and they've come back from the lab. The evidence is thoroughly consistent with a bullet having passed through the bone. It should heal nicely, but I thought I would confirm that for you."

"Thank you. I guess." Jackie laughed. "It's not every day that you adopt a dog with a gunshot wound."

"No—and I just wanted to let you know that it might be a good idea for you to tell the police. I am required to file a report—just like the human hospitals must do—in the event of treating such a case. That's the real reason I wanted to speak to you. To warn you not to be surprised if you hear from the police."

Now Jackie laughed in earnest. "Dr. Huckle, if you only knew," she said at last. "The police are getting to be old friends. Because of the murder here."

"Oh, yes. I forgot that you might be involved in that. I mean—"

"That's all right, Doctor. I know what you mean. Well. Do I have to make out a report or anything?"

"No, I've taken care of the paperwork. Just wanted to let you know. Also, Ms. Walsh, I suggest a heartworm prophylactic if you are intending to keep the dog."

"Right," said Jackie. "Heartworm. Can you send it to me? Or do we need to come in?"

"I can send it right out today."

"Thank you. With a bill, I hope. Anything else, Doctor?"

There was a brief pause, and Jackie heard him draw a deep breath. "Nothing else of a professional nature. That is to say, I have two tickets to the opera for next Thursday. And I wondered if you might be free to join me. That is to say, if you care for opera. And if you're free. And if you don't mind."

Jackie was amused and touched. But she had no intention of dating her veterinarian. They would just break up, and things between them would be awkward, and she'd feel rotten with guilt and have to find another veterinarian. She detested pragmatism in these matters, but there it was. Now: how to get out gracefully?

"Thank you so much, Dr. Huckle. That's very kind of you—but my boy Peter has a hockey match next Thursday, and I really have to be there."

"I see. Quite the little athlete, eh?"

Thank heavens, Jackie reflected. Huckle was taking it like a gentleman. No threat of a backup offer. "He's trying to be. And I'm called upon to be a one-woman cheering section. You know, faithful to the last." Jackie felt a rush of friendly feeling, of the sort that often attends being let kindly off the hook in such matters.

Huckle said good-bye cheerfully, and as Jackie hung up she began to feel rather sorry that she had said no. He was, after all, an attractive man; and it must be tough to meet single women if you were in your dog-and-cat hospital till all hours every day. But on balance, she reflected, it was better to have a good vet than to risk his being a so-so suitor. A bird in the hand. She had done the right thing.

Now all that remained was to speak to Graham Grosset. She reached for the phone and dialed the secretary of the English department. Grosset was teaching a class in Armstrong Hall; the class finished up at about three-thirty. Jackie looked at her watch. Just time to catch him; with any luck she could have his copy of the screenplay in hand for Westfall and the president by four o'clock.

She dashed across the campus to the solid old limestone-and-mortar edifice where the English department held forth, and lurked about outside the door of Room 216 until a gaggle of noisy students emerged. Then she knocked and entered.

Graham Grosset was in many ways a figure larger than life, but physically, he was just about right. He was fifty-five or thereabouts, with very fair skin and a corona of pale red-gold hair that seemed to glow like a nimbus. He wore a loose-fitting suit of fine Kashmiri wool and loafers of soft leather; as Jackie entered the classroom he was adjusting a long, dark, woolen cape that fell from his shoulders to the ground in majestic folds and swept out behind him

as he walked. Jackie had often seen him striding about
the campus in this getup. It had struck her that he looked
almost costumed for the role of the eccentric genius—
except that his genius was altogether real. Jackie felt her
usual composure desert her momentarily.

She quickly introduced herself and explained her errand,
on behalf of B. Crowder Westfall and the president. "It's
all been complicated, because of the police and everything,
and somehow I haven't been able to locate Dr. Barger's
copy of the screenplay. But of course everyone is interested
in making sure the project stays on track, especially the
president. So—I just wondered if Philip might have left
his screenplay with you."

Grosset looked at her in amazement, his pale eyes wid-
ening. "You're not serious."

"I'm afraid so."

"Dear heaven." He snapped a battered brown briefcase
closed and swept out of the room, motioning Jackie to
follow. "Come, child. What about that woman—Patience,
is that her name?"

"Polly. You mean our departmental secretary."

"That one. The precise one, with the nun's clothing."

"Polly Merton. No, apparently she doesn't have it. Barger
didn't let her keep the files, you see. He kept them himself."

"Interesting. I shouldn't have expected that of Philip."
Grosset trotted quickly down the stairs, pausing to hold
open the main door for Jackie. Then he began to walk at
a racing clip; and Jackie nearly had to jog to keep up. As
Grosset walked, he talked. "Philip had a way of running
away from work, as a rule. Handing it off, whenever possible. I noted that tendency in him."

Jackie was obliged to agree, but she did so as coolly as
possible, wanting Grosset to know that her loyalty to her
department was intact. He got her message, but brushed
it aside.

"Don't waste your pretty sentiments on me, my dear. In
the nine weeks since I arrived here, I am afraid I got to

know Philip Barger rather well. The man was a wastrel and a nincompoop. You look like neither of those things, so I suspect you caught a glimmer of his failings. I am perfectly delighted that you can't lay your hands on his odious screenplay; its being lost will save me a good deal of nuisance. Please don't trouble yourself to look for it."

They had reached the intersection of Cuthbert and Walnut streets, and Grosset deposited himself airily on the bench at a bus shelter. His face took on a look of placid patience. "Your American system of transport is so dreadfully backward. I really ought to get myself a bicycle. But then, of course, the hoodlums would simply take it from me."

"I'm sorry, Dr. Grosset—I'm not sure I understand what you mean. About the screenplay, not about the buses."

"I mean, my dear, that I was never keen on the movie project to begin with. Philip Barger talked me into it against my better instincts. He could talk anyone into anything, that man. Missed his calling; should have sold orthopedic shoes for a living. Now that he is dead, however, all bets are off. I am going to behave like a nasty child and insist upon my own way, so I suggest you save your arguments. My books shall remain books. My work shall never again be tainted with the false light of filmmaking; nor shall I ever again be compelled to listen to the sniveling, drooling, infantile mewling of a script writer, director, producer, or actor."

The Number 16 bus arrived with a squeal of brakes, and Grosset swooped up the stairs to deliver his parting shot. "We must all learn to thank our Heavenly Father for the small blessings that He rains down upon us in this tiresome life. Good day, my child."

The bus door swung shut and the vehicle roared away, leaving Jackie speechless in a haze of diesel exhaust.

"What's up, Jackie?" asked a familiar voice. "Miss the bus?"

Jackie turned to see the friendly face of Mark Freeman, the animation specialist. "Missed the boat, Mark."

"What's the matter?"

"Nothing. Really nothing." Jackie thought it best to keep the story of the lost screenplay to herself, for now. "What's up with you?"

"I'm nervous." Mark Freeman grinned, looking anything but nervous. "We're all under suspicion."

"Naturally."

"At least I am, I know. Your friend the police detective came calling last night."

"Oh." Why did everyone insist on thinking that Lieutenant McGowan was her friend? wondered Jackie. She let it slide.

"Fortunately, I was out, and I didn't have to answer all of his impertinent questions about my relations with the other members of the department. But he'll be back tonight. What shall I tell him?"

"About what, Mark?"

"About the huge argument I had with Philip the day he died."

"Are you serious?"

"Serious."

"What did you argue about?"

"My new computer. I found out that he had squelched the deal to buy it—right after I turned down the offer from U.S.C."

"What a stinker. Honestly, that man was a stinker."

"Don't speak ill of the dead, Jackie," said Mark with a laugh.

"I don't hold with that. He was a perfectly horrible human being."

"And then I had the pleasure of a long meeting today with our new chair."

"Our new what?" Jackie felt distracted and out of touch. Graham Grosset had that effect on people, she supposed.

"Our chairwoman. Chairperson. Chair."

"Ah. Merida. What did she have to say?"

"That she's not sure about the future of animation as an art; that the equipment is too expensive; that the product is lowbrow; and that I'm a dilettante."

"Right." Jackie laughed. Mark Freeman had won very high marks in the film world for his extraordinary skill and humor. The film school at U.S.C. had been trying to get him for years; and it was lately rumored that KidVid Studios were after him to create a new series of feature films for general release. He was, in short, a hot property, and everyone at Rodgers knew it. Merida Green must be off her nut.

Jackie expressed this opinion, and did not mince words.

"Well, we all knew that," replied Mark, "but don't forget that she's got a line-item veto on the budget allocations for next year. If I don't get my new computer, after all the waiting and filling out of forms and swearing in blood that the school has put me through, I'll slit my wrists. I promise I will." He gave Jackie a mournful smile. "Or maybe I'll just sulk. But I'll do something."

"I wouldn't let it worry you, Mark." Jackie, however, was worried on her own account. If Merida Green had begun in her new position by attacking Mark Freeman, there was nary a hope that she'd leave Jackie in peace. Jackie was the most junior member of the department, with the exception of David Surtees. She grew uncomfortable at the thought of having to toe the line for Merida, but she did her best to find the humor in the situation. "I guess it's time for me to become a card-carrying Woman in Film, if I value my job."

Mark Freeman nodded, chuckling softly. "A smart move, Jackie. And while you're at it, acquire a few abrasive character traits. Merida likes 'em in her own image."

He headed away, and Jackie, feeling now truly glum, headed for Wescott Hall, where the president and the dean of faculty had their offices. It would be best to take the bull by the horns.

• • •

"Dear me, dear me," prattled B. Crowder Westfall after
Jackie had related the gist of her conversation with Grosset.
"I know genius is supposed to be touchy, but I rather won-
der at the man. I do. He did have an agreement, after all."

"I wouldn't know anything about that," Jackie protested,
hoping to bring her own role in the affair to a quick end.
"He was rather insistent, Dr. Westfall, and I would be
willing to bet that he meant everything he said."

"Stubborn. That's what he is. Been resting on his laurels
for far too long, I'm afraid." Westfall leaned perilously back
in an old wooden armchair, which gave a mighty creak. His
office, with its mahogany-paneled walls and floor-to-ceiling
bookcases, suited him beautifully. His desk was of black
walnut, its top buried beneath heaps of papers, reference
works, dictionaries, and all manner of scribbled-on scraps.
Jackie noted with amusement that there was no telephone
on Westfall's desk—nor could she find one anywhere in the
room. Probably a nod to the ancients, she supposed. Why
were academics always so idiosyncratic?

"I'm sorry I couldn't help more, Dr. Westfall." She began
to rise from her seat, but the dean of faculty waved an arm
in silent protest, and she sat again.

"We must think on this, my dear Mrs. Walsh. The best
solution, of course, would be for that man to come swiftly
to his senses. Failing such a happy ending to our dilemma,
however, we will be forced to deliberate. Which course
of action would be most efficacious, under the circumstances? Your insights and professional standing are invalu-
able. Really. I know nothing about movies, nothing at all."

For God's sake, thought Jackie. *They can't mean to make
me responsible for this whole damn thing.* Her instincts told
her that she might run into some political problems, down
the road, if she put in her oar now.

Besides—she had never really cared much for Philip
Barger; there was nothing she felt she owed the dead man.
Nor would Grosset's reputation have anything significant

to gain from the project as it now stood—his only interest, from the start, really, had been the money. Now Grosset would be free to maintain his curmudgeonly distance from the world of popular culture and the visual arts, having already been paid something, Jackie was fairly sure, as a result of the option. Jackie wondered about the deal. It would have been an interesting angle to explore, if she had actually seen any point in following through on this whole silly mess.

Aloud, Jackie replied to Westfall's probing and urging with a polite but firm refusal. "Unless the script and all the papers turn up," she said, "there is really very little that any of us can do, Dr. Westfall."

"This is dreadful. Terrible," said Westfall, his solemn face looking more hangdog than usual. "Of course I shall be obliged to communicate this news to the president. And of course I shall tell him of your kind willingness to help us find a way to make everyone happy."

There was nothing Jackie could say in protest, so she resigned herself. Fortunately, the president was widely known as a man of small personality and little administrative flair. Jackie hoped he would run true to character and give the whole Kestrel project up as futile.

That evening, Graham Grosset cooked himself a simple but well thought out supper in his small kitchen. By night, at home alone, he seemed a different man. Gone were the effusive gestures that he affected in the daily commerce of life; gone too were the flamboyant clothes that he wore in his role of the eccentric professor. On the stove was a steaming pot of homemade leek soup. He stirred it with an economical movement and put a small loaf of French bread in the oven to warm. He carefully took down a fine, gilt-rimmed soup bowl of bone china from the cupboard, and set a solitary place for himself at the dining table with a spoon, knife and fork of antique French silver. He poured out a glass of red wine, wiping the lip of the bottle with a delicate motion.

When the candles were lighted, he turned on the record player; the Brahms "Academic Festival Overture," which never failed to bolster his spirits. Then he poured out his soup into the fine, gilt-edged bowl, and sat down. He bent his head for a moment; an onlooker might reasonably have concluded that he was saying a brief and silent grace. Then he unfolded his linen napkin, picked up his silver soup spoon, and began to eat.

The telephone gave a dissonant jangle, and with a mutter Grosset set down his spoon and rose to take the call. He glanced at his watch as he picked up the receiver.

"Grosset here."

He listened in silence for ten seconds, then cocked his head thoughtfully.

"I'm afraid I don't follow you . . . Yes, yes." He stared distractedly out the small kitchen window into the moonless night beyond, listening. Eventually, he let out a hearty guffaw. "That's a bloody pipe dream," he said contemptuously. "Where on earth would I get that sort of money?"

The voice at the other end of the phone went on for nearly a full minute. Grosset listened, his air of abstraction increasing. He walked with the telephone over to the kitchen counter and began idly to slice a carrot. His knife was very sharp, and the little rounds of carrot were paper-thin, translucent. You could almost have seen through them.

At last, Grosset gave out a little sigh. "I'll have to consider everything that you've told me. I suppose you wouldn't care to leave a number where I might reach you? . . . No, I didn't think so. Well, righto then. I shall await your call."

He hung up the telephone and padded softly back to his supper. The soup had grown cold; he scowled at the film that had formed on the top, then dipped in his silver spoon, and ate.

CHAPTER 8

"Dugan was on to something, no question about it," said Cosmo Gordon to Lieutenant Michael McGowan. The two men were once more at the Juniper Tavern; it was evening, on a chilly Thursday in November, and there weren't any people in the place. In spite of this fact, however, Cosmo Gordon kept his voice low, and watched the front door of the tavern carefully. "On to something big."

"Oh, come on, Cosmo. I know you liked the guy—"

"Shhh!" Gordon held up both hands and spoke in a quiet voice. "I tell you, Mike, there is something going on in this town."

"I never took you for a conspiracy theorist, Gordon," replied McGowan, taking a long pull at his beer. "Not for a minute. What put this harebrained idea into your head?"

Gordon twisted his bar stool and leaned back easily against the solid, warm length of the mahogany bar. "I thought Dugan was going over the edge. You know—I thought he'd be seeing pink elephants before long. So I didn't pay that much attention to him, the night he came over to our place. Nancy listened more closely than I did. Something about the mayor, or some guy on the mayor's staff, being into the mob for a lot of dough. Sounded either completely plausible, or completely crazy, at the time. Anyhow, I had things on my mind. So I just wasn't all that interested."

"But now you think there was something to it?"

"I'm sure of it. Not a little thing, either—not some political clown who owes the Family a few thousand, or even a hundred thousand. Bigger. We're talking about a major corruption scandal, Mike. Could tear City Hall to pieces."

"Right." Mike McGowan took a swallow of his beer and adjusted the collar of his turtleneck. The two friends sat in silence for a time.

McGowan had a great deal of respect for the police medical examiner, but the young lieutenant was a skeptic about scandal in the modern age. He didn't believe, really, that there was such a thing any longer. No one was truly afraid of being caught; one way or another, it seemed to McGowan, the criminals beat the system nine times out of ten. The threat of having unsavory associations revealed was no real threat at all.

A few minutes elapsed, and McGowan finally put this feeling into words. Cosmo Gordon listened in silence.

Gordon was a member of the old school; he had cut his teeth in the law-enforcement establishment during the administration of Mayor Ward Clement, who had been to Palmer what Fiorello LaGuardia was to New York. In Palmer, such leadership—and the depth of feeling it had aroused—were still keenly felt, twenty-five years later, by those who had known Clement. Michael McGowan was too young to remember.

What was more, McGowan was a different breed of cop altogether. He held a master's degree in criminology, and had studied sociology and psychology in depth. He was much more of a free agent than the old-style cop on the beat. Cosmo Gordon thought the education was probably good for the Palmer police and good for the city, although it generated a kind of questioning intellectuality that made the police force less of an army, and more like a band of roving professors with badges.

Gordon ordered another beer and expressed this view.

"Problem with you, Mike, is that you overintellectualize everything. No clear delineation between right and wrong anymore; everything's got to be embedded in its little network of reasons and excuses."

McGowan took a thoughtful pull on his beer. "Sometimes yes, sometimes no. I'm not a big one on the rights of criminals, you know."

"No? But it always takes you so damn long to define who's a criminal and who isn't, Mike, that by the time you all pull the case together, any ten-dollar lawyer in a shiny suit can get the guys off."

"Hmm."

"Except maybe murderers, right? How's that Barger case coming along?"

McGowan shook his head. "It's not. Not a scrap of evidence anywhere, really. We can't trace the damn key, and the only other people who had a key have alibis. Of a sort, anyway. But talk about your criminals, Cosmo— I'm surprised this guy Barger lasted as long as he did." McGowan had interviewed, in the course of the last four days, no fewer than sixteen former or current Rodgers University students who had had a relationship of one sort or another with the dead film professor. "The guy was a regular whatsit—a regular satyr."

"Didn't know they made satyrs these days. I thought such judgments were a thing of the past." Gordon laughed.

"Definitely qualifies, this guy." McGowan described Barger's house in detail, carefully including in his description a variety of equipment that Jackie Walsh had been either too polite or too sheltered to take notice of.

"You took her with you, Mike?" Gordon laughed again, a hearty chuckle. "Does your superior officer know about this breach of the rules?"

"No way," replied McGowan warmly. "So just keep your mouth shut. She was looking for something that the professor was supposedly working on. A screenplay for some books by that guy Grosset."

"The English guy with the cape and the hats? The one who lives over near us?"

"That's the guy. You ever read his stuff?"

Gordon shook his head. "Never had time for it."

"Personally, I think the guy's a great writer. But I can't figure out how they could make a movie of his Kestrel books. A lot of long paragraphs of description, and you're never sure quite what you're looking at, or doing, because everything is so mysterious."

"Ah—the old blanket of obfuscation routine. I remember it well from my days as an earnest young writer."

"Writer?"

"Polemics for my high-school newspaper. The less you have to say, the more words you get to use. Like that?"

"Yeah. More or less. Some of his books have plenty of action; he deals with historical subjects, so he doesn't really have to make up too much of a plot. If you know what I mean."

"I think I follow you." Gordon smiled, then asked quietly, "You sure she's out of it, Mike?"

"Yup." McGowan didn't elaborate. He would have been hard-pressed to say exactly why he had mentally cleared Jackie Walsh of any involvement in the murder.

"Damn thing about murder," remarked Gordon. "It leaves so many loose ends. Even when there wasn't anything there to start with."

"What do you mean?"

"I mean—look at poor old Matt Dugan. Gunned down behind Leanna's Piano Parlor. His wife and kids long gone; and he lived in a tiny little house, all paid for fifteen years ago, over by that new mall they just put in. Nothing to his life—materially, I mean. Didn't own a car; only had about two shirts to his name. Nothing but him and his damn fool dog. And you know what? The dog's missing."

"Huh. It's always something, I guess." McGowan wasn't interested in Matt Dugan, alive or dead, but he knew how to be polite. "Maybe the dog died or something, and you didn't hear about it."

"No way. Not Alex—or I would have heard about it the other night, when Dugan came by for dinner. No, Alex was fine. Then, poof, he's gone."

"Dogs do that when somebody dies."

"They do, don't they? I think they get disgusted. We let them down."

McGowan rose stiffly and arched his back. "Gotta go. Back to the salt mines."

"Come off it, Mike." Cosmo Gordon looked at his watch. "It's nearly nine o'clock. Why don't you call it a night?"

"No way," replied McGowan, a good-natured twinkle in his eye. "I have a feeling that my pretty little professor is hard at work right now, trying to solve the case. I'll be damned if she's gonna beat me to it."

At eight-thirty that evening, Jackie and Peter returned from a blistering ice-hockey match—the Palmer Mighty Mites had roared past the Tonington Little Devils by a score of 7–3. Peter Walsh, at right wing, had scored an astonishing three goals. After lengthy festivities in the locker room (from which the mothers were fiercely excluded), the crowd of parents and small athletes proceeded to the Tastee Treet stand for a celebration.

As Jackie and Peter arrived home, Jake greeted them with unalloyed joy. He roused himself quickly from his cozy spot under the kitchen table and wagged his tail—stiffly at first, as dogs do when they are just waking up, but then with increasing vigor and flexibility. He really was a most remarkable dog, thought Jackie, watching as Peter covered him with embraces. If he had been on the streets a long time, he must have had a happy home somewhere in his past—he was evidently well able to keep up with the excitement of family life.

Peter went off to bed, and Jackie poured herself a glass of red wine. She sat at the kitchen table, relaxing, stroking Jake behind the ears, and wondering about the Kestrel screenplay. The more she thought about her little interview with Graham Grosset, the stranger his behavior seemed. She fully agreed with his assessment of Barger—what had he called him? A wastrel and a nincompoop. No disagreement there. But how had Grosset mixed himself up with the man in the first place?

Jackie stood up and went to the phone. Her friend, Millicent Brooks, was a professor of English at Rodgers. Millicent knew everything about everybody in the world of letters. She would be sure to have some inside information on Graham Grosset.

The two old friends, who had known each other since childhood, gossiped cheerfully for a while. Millicent, of course, had heard the news of Barger's murder, and pumped her friend for details. Jackie obliged with as many facts as she knew, but there wasn't much to tell.

Millicent Brooks, however, had an interesting sidelight on Barger. One of Barger's former paramours was earning her doctorate in fluid mechanics, under Millicent's husband, John.

Millicent was chuckling. "She told John she really ought to be grateful to Barger. Her experience with him was so awful that she had no choice but to concentrate on her work, to get over the humiliation."

"Nice guy."

"Yeah. He apparently used some kind of blackmail to get her interested."

"Blackmail?"

"Well, basically. You know the routine—'Well, Miss Buxom, the admissions committee for graduate school won't like a poor grade on your transcript. I think we ought to get together and talk about it.' That kind of you-know-what."

"I can believe it," remarked Jackie. "You should see his *house*." She filled her friend in on the negligees and the mirrors and the photographs on the walls. "*Real* attractive and debonair, let me tell you."

"Well, I always say that a good man is hard to find," said Millicent with a giggle. "But really, it's almost not funny. John's student says he was just awful to her. She almost didn't get out of his house alive, once or twice."

"Once or *twice*?" asked Jackie in disbelief. "I would think once was enough. What's the matter with her? Got some kind of a death wish?"

"Nothing like that. She was just trying to get back some things she had left there. Her grandmother's watch, or something. But he wanted to keep it."

"Yikes!" Jackie was really shocked. "That is grotesque."

"Horrible. Truly horrible."

"Well, Millie—how on earth did Philip Barger manage to get his hands on the rights to the Kestrel books? What's the buzz?"

"The buzz is that Barger must have had something on Grosset. Otherwise, no way. No way. Grosset even turned down Merchant Ivory. You know—the E. M. Forster people."

"I didn't realize the properties were so hot. I talked to Grosset about it—"

"*You* did? What'd you think of him? He's really an oddball, isn't he? Our department meetings just haven't been the same since he arrived."

"Well—he's definitely different." Jackie recounted her conversation with the eccentric writer. "So he says to me that Barger was a wastrel and a nincompoop, and of course I can't say anything—"

"Naturally not."

"—but I can't figure out why Grosset got involved in the first place. I thought you might know."

"No. It's a mystery. Probably money—that's what everyone seems to think, at least."

"That's what I figured. All I have to do now is talk the president out of trying to finish the deal." She told Millicent about the missing screenplay.

"Listen," her friend interrupted, "I'll talk to John's student. She might have some idea of where he hides things, where he would have put the stuff."

"That would be terrific. Lieutenant McGowan can't get anywhere with Barger's most recent flame."

"Lieutenant McWho?" Millicent asked swiftly, recognizing a certain tone in Jackie's voice. For another fifteen minutes the two women discussed the police lieutenant—his looks, his marital status, his sense of humor, and his interest in Jackie (which, Jackie was forced to admit to herself, was obvious, and not altogether unwelcome).

The next day Jackie arrived at school to find a note from the president in her mail slot.

"Uh-oh," said Mark Freeman, who had noticed the crest on the stationery and now stood on tiptoes, trying to read the note over Jackie's shoulder. "Fan mail from some flounder?"

Jackie laughed. "No, Bullwinkle. A love letter," she responded, folding the note up quickly.

"What's all this palaver?" asked Merida Green brightly, stepping up to collect her own mail. She glanced with curiosity at the envelope in Jackie's hand, which bore the university president's seal, large as life, in the upper left-hand corner. "A letter from President Obermaier?"

Boy-oh-boy, this woman is nosy, thought Jackie, trying to keep her face expressionless. "Morning, Merida," she replied in a level voice.

"Jackie's getting love notes in her mailbox, Merida," teased Mark. "If you don't watch out, she'll be snapped up again by some man who wants a wife, and you'll have to find someone new to teach 101."

"Mark, stop it," objected Jackie, tucking the note into her large leather book bag. "How are you, Merida?" she asked, glowering at Mark.

"Fine, thank you. Jackie, I'm afraid you and I must have a little talk. Are you free for lunch today?"

"Afraid not. Later, though—how about three o'clock?"

"That will suit me very nicely. In my office." Merida stalked away, and Jackie gave Mark a hard look.

"Be careful, Mark. She doesn't like you."

"I know," said Mark cheerfully. "It goes both ways, though, so my feelings aren't really hurt."

"No—but you just watch out. She'll pull a fast one, and there you'll be."

"At U.S.C. Things could be a lot worse."

"Don't be silly. You hate California."

"Yes, I do," replied Mark speculatively as he watched Merida Green pass through the door to the faculty lounge. "I do hate California. It's so cold and so damp."

"So stop being silly. You belong here."

"Maybe." He shrugged his shoulders. "I don't know who belongs here anymore. Bad enough with Barger—but at least he left everyone alone."

"She'll get over it. Maybe she's even likable, underneath it all."

"No," replied Mark.

"No," agreed Jackie. "But maybe she'll find out that bossing everyone around takes up too much time, and she'll lay off."

"Or else Polly Merton will break her spirit for her."

He left to take his morning class, and Jackie retreated to her office, to respond to the note from the president.

Henry Obermaier, the president of Rodgers University, was a short, fat, balding man in his early sixties. At one point he had been considered quite the thing, although nobody could now recall precisely why, and he had come very close to taking an important post at Yale a few years back. Or so the story went. Jackie, like most of the faculty, considered him a tiresome and ineffectual man, and she heartily wished he had taken the job in New Haven.

Obermaier was widely known as "Harmless Henry" because of his famous inability to stand up to his faculty, students, and staff members. Nobody liked him. The board of trustees found him completely spineless, and the faculty just worked around him. The only time, as a rule, that he intruded into anyone's life was Founder's Day. At this springtime ritual he generally gave a long, boring, and thoroughly asinine speech about the history of the school. The speech always fell on deaf ears. Jackie had only met Obermaier once or twice, by accident, at the faculty club.

But this morning, Harmless Henry had himself written her a note, asking her to visit his office at one o'clock, for lunch, if she were free; Stuart Goodwillie was expected.

Jackie sighed deeply. It was too late to pretend illness for today; and besides, she had a class to teach. Thankful, at least, that she had worn her good black wool dress, Jackie phoned the president's office to say she would be there. Then she marched off to Room 108, where her students awaited her.

Jackie noticed at once that Danielle Sherman was missing from class this morning. As a rule, she wouldn't have given such an absence a second thought, but last night's conversation with Millie had given Jackie's curiosity a tweak. And if her lunch date with the president was any indication, the university wasn't going to let the Kestrel project die without a fight. In spite of her protestations of ignorance, Danielle Sherman probably did know something about the dead man's habits—or about his progress on the screenplay, at least.

When the class was finished (today they were discussing the uses of lighting to create mood in Bergman's *The Seventh Seal*), Jackie spoke to Nadia Pitts, a quiet, dark-haired beauty who often sat with Danielle.

"Nadia, do you have any idea where Danielle is today?"

"No, I don't, Jackie. I can try to reach her, if there's something special that you want to talk to her about." Nadia Pitts tossed back a dark lock. "If it's important."

"I think it *is* important," Jackie replied slowly. "Ask her to give me a call tonight, at this number, would you?" Jackie scribbled her home telephone number on a Post-It and handed it over. "Tonight, if it's at all possible."

"Sure." Nadia took the number and stuffed it in the pocket of her jeans.

"And Nadia"—Jackie stopped her—"could you please let me know if you don't reach Danielle? You can leave a message on the machine."

"Sure. No problem."

Jackie returned to her office to pick up her shoulder bag and headed across campus once more to Wescott Hall. In a few moments, she was ushered into the president's office.

Harmless Henry Obermaier was enfolded in the embrace of a deep leather wing chair, but he leapt up as Jackie was introduced. "Ms. Walsh. Very good of you to come, very good," he proclaimed. He smiled a confused-looking smile and raised his eyebrows in an expectant fashion, giving Jackie the momentary impression that it was she, and not the president, who had arranged for the meeting. Then he seemed to recollect himself; still holding the hand that he had shaken, he led Jackie across the room to another wing chair, where a mass of white hair protruded above a gold-and-black-patterned cashmere blanket. Somewhere within its folds, it soon became clear, there was a very old man.

"Mr. Goodwillie," shouted the president, "I should like to present Ms. Jackie Walsh, an instructor at the Longacre Center."

"What's that?" the man shouted back. Then his pale blue eyes focused on Jackie. "Oh, the girl is here?" He stopped and gave out a little noise, somewhere between a cough and a sigh: "Eh-heh." He glowered at Obermaier. "No need to *shout*, Henry," Goodwillie shouted, then focused again on Jackie; this time there was appreciation in his glance. "Most kind of you to come, my dear. Here, sit over there." He shot out a wrinkly hand from beneath his blanket and pointed to a leather ottoman. "Pull that up close, so we can talk. Eh-heh."

Jackie, with a quick glance back and forth between the two men, swiftly decided that Goodwillie was the man of the hour. Even the aging industrialist seemed to share the view that Henry Obermaier was basically a harmless nitwit. So Jackie did as she was told, drawing the ottoman close to the blanketed billionaire, and leaning in so they could talk.

"I'm here to tell you about the Kestrel project," she said in a clear, well-pitched voice. Jackie's father (dead five years now) had been very hard of hearing most of his life, and she had developed a knack for making herself understood. Henry Obermaier, left to fend for himself, pulled up an uncomfortable-looking ladderback chair and listened as Jackie told Goodwillie the story of the missing script, the lost contracts, and the insouciance of Graham Grosset.

"What the devil?" Goodwillie exclaimed when Jackie reported Grosset's comments. "Man's got a contract," he shouted. "Can't go back on a contract, not if you're a man of your word. Right, my dear? Eh-heh." He reached out a wizened hand and patted Jackie's knee; she bore it well, and blessed the thickness of her dark tights.

"That's what the trustees say," put in Obermaier. "I, er, was just talking the whole thing over with Ashley Landis, our new chairman. Chairwoman. Whatever." Obermaier blinked, opened his eyes wide, and raised his eyebrows again with that quizzical, expectant look. "She agrees."

Jackie drew a deep breath and began to talk in earnest. She explained that the contract between Barger and Grosset had not yet been located; and no one at the Longacre Center seemed to have any idea of what the terms were. Polly Merton claimed that she had had nothing to do with the contract. No one at the university, in fact, had a clue.

Jackie was beginning to give up on getting through to these two men, each befuddled in his own way. Goodwillie's eyes began to glaze over, then his paper-thin eyelids came down like tiny curtains, very slowly, until they nearly covered his eyes. His head began to nod; Jackie glanced desperately toward President Obermaier, whose eyebrows shot up to new heights by way of response.

Jackie returned her gaze to the somnolent billionaire. "So you see, Mr. Goodwillie," she explained patiently, "there isn't very much anyone can do, until we find out where we stand."

Goodwillie's head came up suddenly. "Nonsense!" he shouted. "Next of kin. Eh-heh." He patted Jackie's knee once more.

There was a knock at the door and a stout, middle-aged woman, whom Jackie recognized as Martha Zweiback, the president's secretary, entered. She bore a large tray. Without a word, she placed the tray on a table near Goodwillie's elbow and fetched a trio of small, black lacquer tables (Chinese, by the look of them, thought Jackie, and probably very valuable). Martha Zweiback silently arranged the tables, one before each of the luncheon group, and brought out the food. Jackie was amazed: crab salad, fresh bread, and a very nice bottle of white wine.

The stout woman departed, having never said a word; Obermaier gestured at the meal with an open hand, saying, "Why don't we have a little lunch?"—as though no one else in the room might have thought of doing such a thing. Then he tucked his linen napkin into his shirtfront and reached for his fork.

Jackie was grateful for the distraction. Goodwillie was a dirty old man and Harmless Henry was clearly teetering on the brink of lunacy. Jackie knew there wasn't much more she could tell Goodwillie and the president, but she hated to leave this situation open-ended; she wanted her own involvement to end speedily. The university would have to proceed on its own, without expecting the faculty at the Longacre Center to pick up the pieces.

When everyone had settled in to eat, Jackie told them so, in a polite and deferential way.

"You like that feller?" Goodwillie shouted.

"Do I like Philip Barger?" she asked.

"No, no." Goodwillie waved his fork dismissively in the air, sending little specks of crabmeat flying. "Grosset. D'you like his work?"

"I loved *The Tale of Gorgonzola*," Jackie replied.

"That is a wonderful story," chimed in Obermaier. "Isn't it?"

"Be quiet, Henry," shouted Goodwillie. "I'm talking to the girl." He fixed his watery blue eyes on Jackie. "What did you like about that one, my dear? Eh-heh."

Jackie thought for a moment. "The point of view is so unusual. And there is real wit in it—not slapstick, but enough to keep you chuckling through all the tragedies of the woman's life."

"Precisely!" shouted Goodwillie, banging his fork down hard on the plate. "The droll strumpet, beset with tragedy on all sides, but laughing like Auntie Mame. A charming character. Henry, get this damned food out of here. I've had enough."

Obermaier, in the midst of taking a large bite of his lunch, put down his fork and went to the telephone. He spoke. "Martha. We're all finished in here."

Jackie wolfed down the few remaining bites of her lunch as quickly as possible, then moved to help Martha with the plates; but Goodwillie stopped her. "Sit down, girl," he shouted, "and talk to me about literature and the movies."

So Jackie sat once more, and obliged—as best she could—with a patent discourse on the relationship between the written word and the screen. She talked about the pitfalls and the necessary shortcomings in translating any book into film; and she described one or two very successful movies that had been made from literary beginnings that were only so-so. President Obermaier sat, one knee slightly raised and locked in his clasped hands, his head tilted to one side, and listened with the air of an acolyte.

After fifteen minutes of this, Jackie had had about enough. She glanced at her watch, and then spoke in her best apologetic tone about the lateness of the hour.

"I have a meeting with our new department chair," she said, rising stiffly from the ottoman. "Merida Green. And I really must get myself ready for it. That is, if there's nothing more I can do for you here?"

Goodwillie leaned back in his chair and pulled the black-and-gold blanket all the way up to his chin. "You're a bright, clever girl," he shouted. "You get to the bottom of this, girlie, and I will make it worth your while. So will Henry, here."

"Ah—" Obermaier began, but Goodwillie cut him off.

"Shut up, Henry." He looked at Jackie once more. "If you don't find out what happened to that script, I will cut off my endowment to the university and the Longacre Center. You will bear the responsibility for that loss, I imagine—not officially, but in fact. So I suggest you find out, my dear. Now—how about a little kiss good-bye? Eh-heh."

Jackie beat a swift retreat to the sanctuary of the Longacre Center. She looked at her watch as she hurried through the chilly November air toward her appointment with Merida Green. Right on time—and for once, Jackie was looking forward to talking to the woman. If she had been forced to endure another minute of being petted, patted, cajoled, and threatened, Jackie might have been ready to enroll herself as a member of Women in Film.

The new chairperson pro tem of the department greeted Jackie cordially enough.

"I hope I'm not late, Merida. I was unavoidably detained."

"Lunching with Harmless Henry?"

"How did you know?"

"Come off it, Jackie. You know how Martha Zweiback talks. The word is out that Goodwillie wants to go ahead with the project—Philip's movie."

Jackie nodded. "I've been trying to talk them out of it. Frankly, Merida, the whole thing seems like a major headache."

"You think so?" Merida Green's tone was cool. "It would be a feather in our cap, don't you think?"

"If we can find the script, and if Graham Grosset will cooperate. Two big ifs."

"It's too bad, really. I know that Philip was nearly finished, wasn't he?"

"How should I know?"

"Weren't you here that night?"

Jackie gave her a hard stare. "Not that night, Merida. I left at about six-fifteen."

"Oh. I thought it was later, somehow. Well—no matter. I'm sure that Stuart Goodwillie will get his movie made." She settled her reading glasses on her nose and sniffed. "Well, now. I just thought we ought to catch up on a few administrative details. I see here"—she flipped open a large computer printout—"that you haven't yet submitted the midterm grades to the registrar."

"They're not due until next Tuesday, are they?" asked Jackie, trying to sound friendly.

"No, no. That's true. But you gave your class their midterm assignment a full week ago. At least, that's what Polly Merton's records would seem to indicate. Polly keeps very careful records." Merida squinted through her reading glasses at the printout, running an officious finger down the page.

Jackie refused to squirm. "The assignment was a research paper," she said, "and everyone needs a chance to use the video library. The papers are due tomorrow."

Merida Green looked up, her brown eyes focused over the rim of her glasses at Jackie.

"A paper. Why not an exam?"

"It's a combination—a take-home."

"I see. Don't you think that's letting them off a little bit too easily? Above all, Jackie, we don't want a lot of students signing up for our courses—especially our introductory courses—with the idea that they can get away with—" she broke off.

"With murder?" asked Jackie, a grim smile on her face. "No, I doubt they think so, Merida. Although the idea seems to be catching on with somebody."

"That's not amusing, Jackie."

"It wasn't intended to amuse. You have to admit that the students have had a shock. Especially—" Jackie stopped herself with the thought of Danielle Sherman, absent from class today.

"Especially what? Philip's latest? I wouldn't worry about her, Jackie—she brought it on herself. She had no—" Merida broke off.

"No what?"

"No cause to get herself into such a situation in the first place. Besides—life is full of shocks. The sooner those kids learn to bear up, the better off they'll be. Or don't you agree?"

"Well, of course I agree." Jackie really disliked this woman, and Merida knew it. Jackie was treading on thin ice, administratively speaking. Between Polly Merton and Merida Green her future at Rodgers could be over before it started. But murder or no murder, Jackie stood by her midterm assignment.

She decided to take the offensive. She rummaged around in her book bag and came up with a folded paper. "Here, Merida, is a copy of the assignment that I gave the class." She placed it on the desk. "As you'll see, I've asked them for twenty-five hundred words on two of four questions, each requiring a thorough knowledge of four films. I gave them eight days to see the films and write their responses because there are seventeen students, and there is bound to be a big rush for time in the video library."

"Yes, I see," said Merida sourly. She sat back in her chair, pushed her glasses to the top of her head, and regarded Jackie. "You are still a dispensable member of this department, Jackie."

Jackie swallowed hard and stared at Merida. "Of course. Everyone is, I would imagine."

"Don't imagine. My advice to you is to begin to take your work seriously. And cut out all this behind-my-back politicking with Westfall and Obermaier."

"Merida—"

"I know what you're up to. And it won't work. If you
don't like the way I plan to run this department, I suggest
you begin now to look for work elsewhere. *If* you can find
it. I'm not a person to trifle with, Jackie. I take my career
quite seriously. So don't think that your good-natured airs
will get you where you want to go."

Jackie was beginning to feel that she had suffered enough
abuse for one day. First Goodwillie's slobbering threats,
and now this venomous woman. Jackie remained cool.
"I hate to disappoint you, Merida, but I really am good-
natured. It's not an affectation; I can't help myself. My husband used to complain about it. He called it 'chirpiness.' "

Merida Green snorted, and Jackie went on. "And as for
doing anything behind your back—I really have no ambition, other than to teach my few courses well, and bring up
my child. I have no desire for power in this department. If
you disapprove of my conferences with university administrators, you are welcome to request an invitation. Better
yet, you can attend them in my stead, and I will spend the
afternoons at the movies. I'll speak to the dean of faculty
about your unhappiness, if you like, and he will be sure to
invite you. I'm quite positive nobody meant to hurt your
feelings." Jackie stopped. She felt her face growing red—
always a danger sign. Jackie rarely lost her temper, but
when she blew her stack, she blew it sky-high.

"That's enough, Jackie. See that you have those midterm
grades in on time. And I'd like a copy of all the papers,
when you have graded them."

"Sure," replied Jackie in an amiable tone, "if you'll ask
Polly to authorize the photocopying, I'll get them to your
pigeonhole on Tuesday."

CHAPTER 9

Late that Friday afternoon, Jackie called McGowan. "I really hate to bother you, and I know I sound like a hysterical female or something." Jackie sounded upset, annoyed, and nearly out of breath; McGowan took pleasure in soothing her. She had called *him* in her moment of need.

"Just wait, Jackie. Hang on." Even as he spoke, Michael McGowan was busy detecting. He detected that he had just abandoned using the name "Mrs. Walsh," and with it all pretense at formality in his relations with the woman on the other end of the line. He quickly examined his conscience for motives, found them all in working order, and grinned. "You okay?"

"*I'm* perfectly fine, Lieutenant. Although I won't tell you what kind of day I've had."

"Worse than Monday?"

Jackie laughed bitterly. "No dead bodies—just a bunch of bothersome administrative types who won't leave me alone. That's not why I called, though."

"Oh." Too bad, thought McGowan. He would like to take Jackie Walsh out for a quiet supper and cheer her up. "Then why *did* you call?"

"Well—I'm worried about one of my students."

Briefly she related Danielle Sherman's absence from class. "Ordinarily I wouldn't be worried. But it struck me that she might know something about Philip Barger—about

99

his habits, and so forth—that she doesn't know she knows. You follow me?"

"I do follow you."

Jackie had heard back from Nadia Pitts, the student who had promised to check up on Danielle. "Apparently her roommates haven't seen her in more than twenty-four hours, and she missed a test this afternoon in organic chemistry."

"Uh, Jackie—are you sure this is significant?"

"According to her roommates, she's pre-med and desperate to do well. She might skip a lecture in Film History 101—let's be honest with ourselves—without worrying too much about her future. But not a midterm in organic chemistry."

"They haven't heard from her?"

"Who? The roommates? No. Nobody has heard from her since she went out early last night. She told one of her roommates that she was going to meet someone, but didn't say who. And that she'd be back for dinner later on, maybe with something interesting to tell."

"She said that?"

"Yes. The roommate I spoke to—Lynn someone—says Danielle is a bit of a daredevil. Always likes to go out on a limb to prove a point. I'm worried. I think she knew something, and she may be in some kind of trouble."

McGowan had begun to share Jackie's alarm. "All right. I'll check with missing persons, and have someone get over there to take a look around. Where does this girl live?"

Jackie gave him the address, an apartment off campus, not a dorm. "Thank you so much, Lieutenant. I'm sure you think I'm an absolute idiot to get so worked up—"

"Not at all. You feeling better?"

"Much better. Thanks. Will I hear from you soon?"

"Sure. Very soon." Michael McGowan smiled and rang off. He strolled out of his tiny cubicle of an office and made his way down a busy corridor to a small, cramped room; over the door was a dusty, hand-lettered sign that read "Lost and Found."

To fat Sergeant Woltzer in Missing Persons (known universally as the Meatball), McGowan related the particulars of his conversation with Jackie. "Any word about her, Sergeant?"

The Meatball scratched his grizzled head. "Nope. None at all. We got nothing happening in here. You want I should look for her?"

"Of course. What do you think the public pays you for, Meatball?"

"Okay." The fat sergeant pulled a terrible-looking pencil out of a stained coffee cup on the top of his desk and began to make out a report.

This activity took some time; the fat sergeant didn't file many reports, and apparently his idleness had caused him to forget how to write. McGowan coached him patiently.

When the report was finished, the fat sergeant sat back, contented. "It'll be good to have something to do around here. Hardly anybody bothers with Missing Persons anymore. Either people are alive and in somebody's face, or they're dead. No more in-between types, like we used to get in the good old days."

"Before they took adultery off the books, you mean," McGowan said. He had heard legendary tales of mysterious disappearances and passionate elopements, but the Meatball was right. Those had been the good old days. Husbands, wives, and lovers never bothered to run away anymore; and even fewer people bothered to send out a search party. "Hey, listen, Meatball. If you're bored"—McGowan reached in his pocket and pulled out a folded-up piece of paper—"try to find out who this guy is." He handed over the paper.

The Meatball unfolded the paper and examined the image with care. "Yo!" he exclaimed at last. "This isn't a missing person."

"Right, for ten points. Why don't you see if you can track him down? I'd take it as a personal favor."

The Meatball scratched his head. "Okay. But it's a favor, and you owe me."

"Right." McGowan, feeling very pleased with himself, headed back down the hall to Homicide.

Philip Barger's attorney leaned back in the leather wing chair from whose depths, just the day before, Stuart Goodwillie had petted and cajoled and insulted Jackie Walsh. The attorney, Silas Holcombe, bore on his face a look of patient superiority as Harmless Henry Obermaier listened to an account of the disposition of Philip Barger's affairs.

"You see, because Barger died intestate—without a will, if you follow me—his personal effects will pass, according to the laws of the state, to his next of kin."

"Aha!" exclaimed Henry Obermaier, a vacant smile on his face.

"As for his professional effects, however—any papers, films, books, and so forth—Barger did leave a letter of instruction stipulating that all rights in and to such properties be passed to Rodgers University, with the proviso that the university, on receipt of this most generous bequest, rename the film library."

"Rename it?"

"Yes. The 'Philip Barger Memorial Library of Cinematic Arts.' Rather a simple request."

"Oh. Dear me." Henry Obermaier shook his round little head and did his best to explain. "I'm afraid that may be impossible. You see, our library was named for Sabin Hughes, whose family gave the money for its construction. So it would be impossible, really. Not a possibility. Legally. We could name something *else* for Philip Barger, I suppose."

The lawyer shook his head. "The terms are rather specific. You must conform to them before any of the rights to Barger's papers pass to you."

Obermaier scratched his chin thoughtfully. "There is someone whose advice I should like to ask." He raised his eyebrows as though to ask for Holcombe's approval, then rose and shook the lawyer by the hand. "I'll call you shortly to let you know."

When Holcombe was gone, Harmless Henry Obermaier reached for the telephone and called Ashley Landis, the chairman of the board of trustees. Ashley would know just what to do. She always did.

"What?" asked Ashley Landis with a laugh when Obermaier had outlined his idea. "Rename the film library so we can get our hands on that hack's drivel?"

"I know, I know. It's absurd, but what else can we do?"

"We can forget about it. The whole thing."

"But, Ashley—"

"What? I doubt that man ever did any work at all. If he'd asked us to dedicate a pornography museum, I might have thought he'd earned his fame. But not our film library."

"But, Ashley—"

"The answer is no, Henry. I don't see any reason at all to comply. We don't need whatever it is that that man had. I refuse to desecrate the memory of Sabin Hughes for such a farce."

"But, Ashley—"

"But me no buts, Henry. You know as well as I do that the man was probably done in by some jealous mistress. It would be unseemly." When Ashley Landis wanted to close a subject, she tended to talk about what was seemly and what was not.

The pressure was just too much for Harmless Henry. He began to lose his temper. "Ashley, let me just say one thing. Will you?"

"All right, Henry. One thing, and that's it. I'll give you thirty seconds."

"Stuart Goodwillie. If we rename the film library, we own the rights to the Kestrel script. And if we own the rights, Goodwillie will go ahead with his plans for the new endowed chair in your father's memory."

"Ah," said Ashley Landis. All was now simple. "Yes. And all we need is to find someone to finish up that stupid project."

"Yes, yes," clucked Harmless Henry. "I have just the person."

"I'll present the idea to the board on Monday."

CHAPTER 10

Lieutenant McGowan had a call from the Meatball on Saturday afternoon. When the phone rang, McGowan was sifting restlessly through the file on the Barger murder, wishing he were at the gym, or the hardware store, or the movies—anywhere but his untidy office at Palmer Central, faced with a dead professor, a missing woman, and nothing to go on. Nothing.

He grabbed for the telephone as it rang. "McGowan, Homicide."

"Yeah, Lieutenant. Sergeant Woltzer here."

"Hey. How's it goin', Meatball?"

"Good. Yeah. Well, look. I got a make on your request of earlier in the week."

McGowan sat up, alert. "The Sherman girl?"

"No, no. Nothing about the girl. The other one, your buddy. The dog."

"Oh."

"Yeah. You're not gonna believe this. You know how they say it's a small world. Like, they say, if *you* know somebody that *I* know, then we say, 'Small world.' "

"We sure do, Meatball."

"So, there's dogs and there's dogs. This one, of course, is a German shepherd."

"I was told it was an Alsatian shepherd."

"Same diff."

"You sure?"

" 'Course. So listen. Here's the poop, if you forgive my little joke." The Meatball laughed, a low growl of a laugh, punctuated by a hiccup.

McGowan took a deep breath. Why wasn't there a bar at the station house? He could use a frosty beer right now.

"I'm kinda surprised at you, Lieutenant. Didn't recognize one of our own."

"Huh?"

"K-9. The Palmer force. This here"—the Meatball scrutinized the flyer—"is Alexander the Great, better known as Alex. Served with distinction for seven years. Then a few years back he got pensioned off, went to live with Matt Dugan."

McGowan's feet hit the floor with a loud slap. "Dugan? You sure about this?"

"Sure, Lieutenant. I brought that paper you gave me down to Palmer South. Thought I'd show it to Cornelius, maybe he'd know where to start looking." Cornelius Mitchell was the dog handler for the Palmer police. "He took one look and says 'That's Alex.' "

"No fooling."

"He says he's sure it's Alex, but he wants to see him in person, so to speak—heh, heh, heh—and check it out. Says it's too much of a coincidence, you showing up with this dog right after Alex went missing. Been missing ever since Dugan got shot, a week ago."

"Right, I know."

"Mitchell wants all the details. So will Captain Healy, when he hears about it."

"Yeah, yeah . . . Just keep it under your hat until I talk to you again, okay, Meatball?"

"Why? The name and address is right on the paper."

"Just hang on. Going to do a friend a favor. All right?"

"Yeah, sure. Sure."

"Thanks, Meatball. I owe you one."

"You sure as hell do."

McGowan hung up, grabbed his jacket, and headed for

Isabella Lane. He wanted to give Peter and Jackie Walsh the news in person.

Thus it was that Lieutenant McGowan was away from his desk when the call came from Cosmo Gordon, who had just completed a cursory examination of a fresh corpse.

Jackie and Peter were climbing out of their Jeep when McGowan pulled up. Jackie gave him a grin.

"Detect anything yet, Lieutenant?"

"I have some news for you," he said, hefting a large brown bag of groceries from Jackie's arms and following her up the steps to the front door.

"About that dead guy?" asked Peter, feeling a thrill. He was very proud of his mother's role in the discovery of the corpse.

"About your dog."

"Oh." Peter blinked.

Jackie glared at McGowan and opened the door wide. "After you."

"Relax," urged McGowan. "It's good news. At least, I think it's good news."

"Hooray!" shouted Peter, dancing about the kitchen. He darted to the back door and opened it wide. "Jake!"

Jake let out a short, loud bark of greeting and hustled into the kitchen. He sniffed at his bowl and then submitted to an embrace from Peter, who ruffled the thick black fur about the dog's neck and planted a kiss on his long nose.

"Here he is," said Peter needlessly. "Now you can tell us."

While Jackie put away the groceries, McGowan related the Meatball's findings.

"When the dog retired," said McGowan, after explaining how the connection was made, "he went to live with a, er, a retired cop. Who died recently." McGowan thought it best to omit the circumstances of Dugan's death. No point in burdening Jackie Walsh with too many murders at once. "We'll probably need to take him by the K-9 office, have him looked at. But Cornelius Mitchell was sure it's Alex. And he should know—he trained him."

"Not Alex. Jake," corrected Peter, looking at the dog carefully. Alex wasn't a bad name, either. But he would stick to Jake.

"Jake," agreed McGowan.

"And he's a police dog?" asked Jackie.

"Retired. Technically, though, I think he's still City property—an official member of the Force, you might say." He leaned up against the counter, folded his arms, and grinned at Peter.

"Wow," said Peter, looking with admiration at Jake. "Wait till I tell Isaac. He doesn't have a real police dog!"

"Peter, honey, if Jake belongs to the police, we may not be able to keep him," said Jackie carefully. "He's not really ours, you know."

"But, Mom! The guy's not even alive anymore. Jake belongs to us now."

Jackie shot a look at McGowan. "Great. So now what do we do? Give him back?"

"I think I may be able to pull a few strings. If you'd like."

Jackie smiled her thanks. "I think we'd like, all right."

"In fact—" McGowan looked at his watch. "Can I use your phone?"

"Of course, Lieutenant." Jackie gestured to the telephone on the wall.

McGowan called Palmer South and spoke to Cornelius Mitchell, the K-9 handler, who was still talking to the Meatball about this and that. Mitchell agreed to look at the dog on Monday and, if Jake proved to be the same dog that Matt Dugan had adopted, to take whatever steps might be necessary to transfer the adoption to Peter Walsh.

"One more phone call," McGowan said, dialing Cosmo Gordon's number. Cosmo's wife Nancy answered.

"He's not here, Mike. But he left a message; he wants you to call him. He's down at his office."

"His office?" He glanced toward Jackie, who was open-ing a can of tuna fish. "Thanks, Nancy. I'll head over there. Tell him if he calls, will you?" He hung up.

"Would you like to have some lunch, Lieutenant?" asked Jackie.

"Afraid I can't." McGowan felt a real pang of regret. But he had a feeling that something was up. "Can I take a raincheck?"

"Sure thing. The least we can do for you is to feed you a sandwich, if you can help us adopt Jake."

"Uh—you could do one other thing."

"Name it, Lieutenant." Jackie gave him a big grin.

"Call me Michael." He smiled at her, said good-bye to Peter and Jake, and headed downtown to the medical examiner's office.

Peter Walsh spent the rest of that Saturday afternoon with Isaac, in a small park near Isaac's house, putting Jake through some paces. Isaac's own dogs—three mutts of varying sizes and degrees of scruffiness—were left at home while the two boys tested out a theory—to wit, that Jake was an exceptional dog that could do almost anything. Peter was strongly in favor of this view; Isaac still had deep doubts.

The fetching exercises went much as they had gone before, leaving Peter slightly disappointed in his dog. Isaac had brought along a Frisbee, and Peter a tennis ball; and although Jake displayed a great willingness to oblige his small master, there was no eagerness apparent as he loped after these missiles, and their retrieval clearly brought very little satisfaction to any of the parties involved. It was a chore, performed amenably enough, but with no heart.

"He's a *working* dog," Peter said, for the ninth or tenth time. "He doesn't really know how to play dog games. But I bet if we figured out some work for him, he'd be really good at it."

"Yeah, like what kind of work?" asked Isaac, doubtful.

"Maybe he could pull our sled in winter."

"No way." Peter sounded disgusted. "He's not that kind of dog. He needs to do real work—you know—like sniffing out bombs and stuff."

"We don't have any bombs."

"Drugs, then."

"*Or* drugs. That's dumb." Isaac gave Jake a long, hard stare. "See, the problem with having a police dog is that he doesn't know how to be a *regular* dog."

"Yes, he does." Peter put his arms tightly around Jake's neck. Jake licked the boy's face. "Plus, he knows how to be a police dog." With a sudden movement, Peter stripped off his navy-blue pea jacket. He walked over to a young, small pine tree and carefully selected a low branch, about three feet from the ground. He stripped off some of the needles and slid the branch in through one sleeve of the jacket and out through the other. The pea jacket now hung in a fair imitation of a body.

"What are you *doing*?" snapped Isaac. He trotted over to Peter.

"You'll see. Give me your sweater."

Isaac pulled off his sweater—a colorful, thick, hand-knit gem that his mother had made for him—and gave it to Peter.

"We're gonna do an experiment," said Peter. He rolled Isaac's sweater into a ball, then took the woolen scarf from around his own neck and used it to tie the balled-up sweater to the top of the branch.

"It's an effigy," said Peter, proud of his handiwork as well as his vocabulary. He looked down at Jake, who had settled himself casually upon the grass to watch the progress of the experiment. "Right, boy?" asked Peter.

Jake let out a short bark.

"Okay. Now, we go back this way. Come, Jake." Peter led Isaac and Jake to a spot about twenty yards from the pine. "Sit," he told the dog.

Jake sat, his ears alert and his eyes traveling back and

forth between Peter and the dummy on the pine tree.

"This is how they train them," said Peter, who actually had no idea at all about police-dog training. He moved to one side and held Jake by the collar with one hand, stroking his head with the other. "Good boy, Jake. Good boy."

Jake, his attention now focused on the dummy, let out a noise somewhere between a growl and a whine. Then he barked again, his muscles tensing.

Peter let go of the collar. Jake stood up and took half a step forward, then he waited. Peter and Isaac could feel the tension.

"Okay, Jake," said Peter in a slow but authoritative tone. "Ready?" Peter pointed at the dummy. *"Go!"*

Jake bounded across the clearing, and in four long strides had reached the dummy. The boys watched in silent amazement as the dog made a leaping grab for the right sleeve of the pea jacket. His long, sharp teeth closed on empty fabric, and he gave it a tug. Then he let go, bared his teeth, sat back, and snarled at the limp dummy.

"Wow." Isaac was impressed.

Peter poked him with an elbow. "See, I told you." He grinned, proud of his dog. "Let's try this. *Get him, Jake!*" cried Peter.

With a short, vicious-sounding snarl, the German shepherd leapt for the neck of the jacket. He seized the scarf with hungry jaws, and the pine branch gave with a snap. Within seconds, Jake had the jacket pinned to the ground. He stood over it, paws planted firmly on the jacket's shoulders, and growled fiercely down at Isaac's balled-up sweater.

"Holy moley!" exclaimed Isaac.

"Good boy, Jake," called Peter. "Okay. Enough. Good boy. Come." Peter let out a sharp whistle.

Casting a last intimidating look at the recumbent dummy, Jake backed off slowly. He made his way carefully back toward the boys, stopping after every step or two to look back at the heap of clothing on the ground, keeping an eye on it. When he reached Peter's side, he sat down and regarded the still form on the ground.

"See?" said Peter triumphantly. "We just needed to find the right tricks for him to do. Good boy, Jake."

Isaac retrieved his sweater and looked at it. "Great. My mom's gonna kill me," he said, disgusted.

CHAPTER 11

On Saturday night, after supper, Jackie and Jake and Peter went out into the cold November air. They talked contentedly of hockey games, and this and that, as they made their way to Isaac Cook's house, to apologize in person for the destruction of Isaac's hand-knit sweater. Most boys might have kept silent about the day's events, but Jackie wasn't surprised when Peter confided in her. She knew that the boy's father, Cooper, was the reason.

Peter, when still a very small boy, had had an instinct about truth-telling. Long before Jackie had suspected that her husband was unfaithful to her, Peter had taken to grilling him about his activities, in a voice full of false playfulness. Peter had known, or sensed, that all was not right—many months before Jackie had known. The truth had always been vitally important to Peter. He had yet to learn, however, an effective way to elicit it from people; his constant questioning had merely caused Cooper to withdraw from his son. Jackie hoped that Peter would learn to be more effective, over time.

In the meantime, Peter seemed worried that his dog might be blamed for the mishap.

"Uh, Mom. Jake didn't *mean* to ruin it, you know."

"Of course I do, sweetie. But we can't just go around using Isaac's sweaters for Jake to practice on. Right?"

"I guess so."

Jackie chuckled. "Or we *could*—if nobody minded. But

113

it sounds to me like Isaac was sort of upset about it."

"Yeah—well, I guess he thought his mom might be mad. He didn't care too much, though."

"Well, don't tell his mother that. You might hurt her feelings."

"Yeah. But you should have *seen* Jake!" Peter launched once more into a vivid description of the dog's fierceness. Jackie felt a shiver run up her spine. For the first time since Jake had come to live with them, she began to be concerned about his appropriateness for their household. The dog seemed well adjusted enough—but what did they know about Jake, really? All the character testimonials in the world couldn't erase the fact that he had spent the greater part of his life as a police dog.

And what about that bullet wound? Perhaps Jake had been psychologically affected by the attack, and was now just coolly biding his time, like some canine Hannibal Lecter, before turning on the ones he seemed to love. Dogs did go crazy, Jackie knew that for a fact. She shivered, and tried to listen cheerfully to Peter's account of the day's glories.

When they arrived at the Cooks' residence, Isaac's three dogs, roused from their backyard slumber, set about howling and barking up a storm.

"We've come to apologize," said Jackie, raising her voice above the din, when Sarah Cook answered their knock.

"Don't be silly," replied Sarah in a near shout. "Come on in." She held open the door.

"Can Jake come in, Mrs. Cook?" asked Peter. "I promise he'll be really good."

"Sure, Peter. You guys run upstairs with Isaac. Just don't let him near my closets." Sarah Cook chuckled amiably. "And tell Isaac not to let our dogs in!" she called as Peter and Jake ran up the stairs. She led Jackie to the family room at the back of the old house.

Jackie looked around with appreciation. Every wall was covered with Sarah's paintings and drawings, which were—like Sarah herself—pretty and neat, with an underlying edge of humor. Low bookcases ran around the room like wainscoting, their shelves bulging with well-thumbed volumes. In a leather armchair in a corner Sarah's husband Paul—a tall, handsome, bearded man with sparkling green eyes—was reading; he puffed on an old pipe, and the rich scent of the pipe tobacco hung cozily in the air. The Cooks, Jackie reflected, were the perfect academic couple: attractive, smart, and well read, but at the same time, unpretentious and at ease with themselves. It was a rare combination, in Jackie's experience; so many of the faculty couples she knew were neurotic show-offs. Paul and Sarah were a breath of fresh air.

Paul waved a hand. "Hey there," he said, rising. He pointed to his book. "Do you like Dumas? I'm halfway through *The Three Musketeers.*"

Sarah chuckled and her blue eyes lit up. "He's always halfway through that book. He can never bear to finish it. As soon as he does, he starts it all over again."

Jackie smiled. "I've never read it. But my ex-husband was that way about *The Decline and Fall of the Roman Empire.*"

"That's more my style," remarked Sarah. "Although, for books about Rome, I like the Claudius books even better. Juicier stuff, poison and treachery and all that."

"Kind of like life at the Longacre Center, if you ask me," remarked Paul with a twinkle.

"Paul," said Sarah in a warning voice. "That's Jackie's department you're talking about."

"I bet she knows it too," replied Paul. "Or am I wrong? Is everything in your department a bed of roses?"

"Hardly," replied Jackie. "But I hope we aren't quite as far gone as the Roman empire under Caligula."

"Not quite there yet, eh?" Paul Cook chuckled.

"No. But now that you mention it, there is a fair amount of ruthless ambition around, I have to admit. If our new department chair gets her way, I bet I'll be out of a job, pretty quick."

"Uh-oh. Run-in with the authorities?" asked Sarah.

"Maybe they heard you're keeping a killer dog in your house," put in Paul with a laugh.

"I wish that were it. No, unfortunately this woman is out for blood. *My* blood." Jackie described her Friday afternoon conference with Merida Green.

"I know her. Not well—met her a few times, I should say," remarked Paul. "She came to a lecture I gave. 'Undiscovered Portuguese Masters of the Romantic Novel.' "

"That doesn't sound like Merida Green to me," replied Jackie. "She's more the performance art/fem-lit/politically aware type. 'Untempered Voices From the Edge.' You know."

"That's more or less how she struck me. Strident—and not particularly interested in Portuguese literature."

"I guess she wanted to try to open her mind," said Jackie, doing her best to sound polite.

"Without much success," said Sarah with a laugh.

"Did she like your lecture anyway?" asked Jackie.

"I guess so. She didn't actually walk out, but that would have been rude. There were only three takers, in fact, which was a little bit of a problem." His green eyes shone with amusement. "Made the public-address system a bit redundant."

"Look on the bright side," said Sarah. "You're the living authority on undiscovered Portuguese masters of the romantic novel."

"See what a wonderful helpmate I have in my wife?" Paul asked Jackie with a smile. "She always knows exactly what to say." Paul lit his pipe again. "So, Jackie, tell me. Why did your department head get himself murdered?"

"God. Isn't it awful? I haven't got a clue."

"Neither do the police," Sarah put in. "By the way, Jackie, who's the cop that hangs around the film center?"

"He's the detective on the case. His name is McGowan."

"You were seen having lunch with him at the cafeteria this week."

"Oh." Jackie felt her face redden. "He uses me for his departmental source."

"Oh, good," said Paul, puffing hard. "As long as he's just *using* you—"

"Quiet, Paul," said Sarah, scowling jovially at her husband.

Paul grinned. "So I guess you're not a suspect, Jackie. You didn't make the cut."

"I sure hope not. No," Jackie added. "I think they've gotten over suspecting me. Either that, or they've planted that dog of ours as some kind of elaborate in-house surveillance unit." She told the Cooks the story of Jake's origins, as far as was known. "That's why the boys were up to no good in the park this afternoon. I'm really sorry about the sweater, Sarah."

"Don't give it a thought. Isaac was busting out of it anyway. He grows about an inch a week these days."

"At least you have protection," mused Paul. "You ought to take him to class with you, Jackie. Get the recalcitrant students to mind, pretty quick."

"And then some," Jackie agreed. "You ought to have seen Peter's jacket when he came home. The whole right sleeve is torn to shreds."

Paul Cook was determined to stick to the interesting issue of the campus murder. "You must have some idea who did the man in. Especially if you're thick with the police these days. We promise we won't spill the beans. Just tell us what you think."

"Frankly, I don't know what to think. Philip Barger wasn't a particularly nice or good man, and I imagine there are people who think he got what he deserved."

"Plenty of young women—and not-so-young women, for that matter," said Paul.

"Oh, come on, Paul. You don't know anything about it. That's just gossip." Sarah looked sternly at Paul.

"I hate to say it, but Paul's probably right," said Jackie. "You know how jealousy can rankle. And Philip *did* earn his reputation. But if he was murdered by some disgruntled former mistress, why wait until now?"

"Maybe a disgruntled *present* mistress," suggested Sarah.

"Now we're getting somewhere," agreed Paul. "He did have a new girl for the semester, didn't he?"

"Oh, yes. A young woman in my film history class. She may have hated him," agreed Jackie in a thoughtful voice. She related her conversation with Danielle. "She didn't turn up for class yesterday. I don't know whether she hadn't finished her midterm, or whether she thought I would bug her with questions about Philip."

"Hard to tell," agreed Sarah. "Generally, though, if a student is absent from class on the day that a paper is due, it's a safe bet that the paper isn't finished."

"That's what I thought. But her roommates don't know where she is, either."

"Maybe they're just not saying. Out of loyalty."

"Possible," agreed Jackie, considering this option. "If something had happened to her, I think I would have heard by now."

"Right. So relax." Sarah rose. "I have the perfect thing to relax with. Chocolate chip cookies. Any takers?"

Paul and Jackie nodded. "And a glass of milk, Sarah, my love," added Paul. "Milk all around. Right, Jackie?"

Jackie Walsh was deep in thought. "What? Oh—milk would be terrific. Thanks, Sarah." She stared into space again.

"Worried about her, are you?" asked Paul as Sarah headed to the kitchen.

Jackie nodded. "I think she knows *something*, but I

don't think she knows what she knows. If you know what
I mean."

"Most undergraduates are like that, in my experience,"
said Paul.

CHAPTER 12

In a small, tile-walled room at the Palmer mortuary, the lights were burning brightly. They burned from all angles—in bunches overhead and in sconces along each wall—throwing a confusing assortment of thin, pale, overlapping shadows on the pale green tiles of the walls and the dull-looking linoleum of the floor.

As Cosmo Gordon moved about the unmoving figure on the cold metal examination table, multiple ghostly shadows aped his gestures. Now there were three Gordons, now four, who dabbed and peered and poked and muttered over the body on the table. He lifted an eyelid and peered into an unseeing eye. He shook his head at a length of rubber that had been tied, tourniquet fashion, above the elbow of the left arm.

Finally, with a sigh, Gordon removed his surgical gloves and wiped his brow on the sleeve of his blue gown.

"I don't like it," he remarked to his assistant, Lee Humphries.

The young woman nodded. She knew what he meant. "It would have had to be a *large* overdose, don't you think? If she died of an overdose at all."

Gordon nodded. "Offhand, I'd say she doesn't look much like a user. Good skin tone; general health apparently good." He stooped once more over the body. "And there are no needle marks, except the one."

"There's a first time for everything."

"A first time for everything," Gordon repeated. "So there is, so there is." Gordon rubbed his eyes tiredly, then held open the door to the examining room. "A full workup, Doctor," he remarked. "With a lab report. Check that cranial fracture carefully. And pay special attention, would you, to the tissue surrounding the larynx. Any sign of contusion there should be most carefully noted."

"Yes, sir."

"Good. I'll expect your report in the morning." He stepped out of the grisly, antiseptic room and went down the hall toward his own cramped little office, where he found Michael McGowan awaiting him. Gordon reached for the notes he had made and tossed them to McGowan.

"There's your missing witness," said Gordon. He plopped down into his chair with a sigh.

McGowan read the report in silence. Young female Caucasian, age about nineteen. The body had been discovered late in the afternoon behind a dumpster in the parking lot of the Blue Jay, a bar and pizzeria three blocks from the heart of the campus.

The girl had been tentatively identified, from the ID card in her wallet, as Danielle Sherman, a sophomore at Rodgers University.

The Blue Jay's parking lot was well known to police as a favorite haunt of Palmer's drug dealers—a seedy intrusion of the crime-ridden slums that bordered the campus. Next to the body, police had found a used hypodermic syringe containing traces of some kind of solution; an empty plastic packet and a small metal spoon had been discovered a few feet away.

"Not good," remarked McGowan when he had finished reading the report.

"You could say that," replied Gordon dryly. "But look on the bright side. This doubles your chance of finding your murderer."

"You think so?"

"Bound to. This is Barger's girlfriend, am I right?"

"That's it."

"Not a chance that the two killings are a coincidence."

"There's always the chance."

Gordon shook his head. "Nope. I don't believe in it, and neither do you. My feeling is that the girl was knocked out, then injected, and finally asphyxiated. Three simple steps to death."

"Did you find evidence of an assault?"

"Lee Humphries is looking into it now. We'll have a postmortem report by morning at the latest, I expect, although some of the lab information may take a bit longer. But I have little doubt of what we'll find. The lab is at work on the syringe and the other stuff." A look of distaste crossed Gordon's rugged face. "No matter what they find, I think we'll discover something more."

"You think our killer lured her there."

"Sure. Or lured her somewhere, killed her, and then dumped the body."

"I would go with that. In my experience, the Rodgers students don't tend to hang out at the Blue Jay. That neighborhood is pretty rough, and the students stick closer to campus, unless they're looking for trouble."

"You talked to her last week. Did she strike you as the type to look for trouble?"

"There's no doubt she was adventurous. But not the Blue Jay type." McGowan rose to go. "By the way—before I forget. I think I've found Matt Dugan's dog."

"Hah."

"Serious." McGowan related the tale, carefully refusing to acknowledge the grin on Gordon's face. "You were his friend, Cosmo. You see any problem with letting the boy keep the dog?"

Gordon shook his head. "Not unless Cornelius Mitchell finds something to object to."

"Good."

"Or unless we need to use the dog to find Matt's killer." Gordon grinned wryly. "So far, our good Captain Healy's got exactly zero. Can't spare the men for the job, I hear. That dog might be our best bet."

"Right. We'll put together a lineup of known gangsters, and the dog will give us a make. The only problem being that the evidence of a dog won't buy you a pound of Gaines Burgers in a court of law. It ain't admissible."

"Sure it is. A police dog is a *police* dog." Gordon scratched his head. "I think."

"You'll have to reinstate him on the force, then."

"Yeah. 'Raise your right paw and repeat after me.' Well, as far as I'm concerned, your girl and her little boy can keep him till we swear him in again."

"Right. Let me know as soon as you get the postmortem, will you? Meantime, I'll put some people on the Blue Jay parking lot, see what we can dig up in the way of tire tracks, witnesses. The works."

McGowan, feeling deeply troubled, took his leave.

On Sunday morning, Jackie Walsh was catching up with herself after an arduous week, being deliciously and self-consciously lazy. She was aware that the day outside was bright and crisp, but Jackie had no intention of making the best of it. Today, she would do nothing at all.

Peter's father had come by at seven-thirty to take the boy on a day-long fishing expedition, and at nine o'clock Jackie was in her living room, luxuriating with the Sunday newspaper and a third cup of coffee. Jake was lying on the floor beside the sofa, stretched out in an attitude of sleepy mastery. Jackie looked at the dog. Her fears of the day before melted away. There was nothing threatening in this animal; and she supposed she should be grateful that he knew how to be fierce. The neighborhood wasn't exactly the safest in Palmer—although what place was safe, these days? Her little colonial house out in Kingswood had been equipped with a sophisticated alarm, and still Peter's bicycle had been taken right out of the garage, causing tears to flow in abundance.

The telephone rang. Without stopping to think, Jackie answered it, and was instantly sorry.

"Ah, Mrs. Walsh. Dr. Westfall here. Good morning to you."

Jackie cursed silently. Why had she picked up the phone? The last thing she needed was someone else making claims on her. It was difficult enough to balance the needs of her son, her students, and the dog. "Good morning, Dr. Westfall." What on earth did B. Crowder Westfall, dean of faculty, want with her on a Sunday morning?

"I'm most frightfully sorry to bother you at home, my dear," said B. Crowder Westfall in his old-fashioned, cultivated tone, "especially on your day of rest. It's a lovely morning."

"Yes, it is," Jackie agreed, looking vaguely out the window at the sunshine and blue sky beyond.

"Yes. But I did hope to catch you before you set out on any kind of foray this morning. Do you have a moment to chat?"

"Of course. What can I do for you?" She gathered up the telephone and dragged it across the room, settling once more into the sofa. Then she listened.

What Jackie could do, it emerged, was to try once more to talk to Graham Grosset, and to take up the reins of the Kestrel screenplay. In a mellow voice, which sounded untouched by the modern world, Westfall outlined the situation regarding the disposition of Barger's papers. Without actually saying anything specific, he adroitly alluded to the collusion between President Obermaier and Ashley Landis in the matter of the proposed Goodwillie endowment. And he neatly sidestepped the notion of pressuring Jackie in any way—all the while making it clear that her career might well hang in the balance.

"I do think this is a task for which you are well suited, my dear Mrs. Walsh," purred Westfall. "You see, the board of trustees is most impressed indeed by your previous career as a writer of screenplays. You have done quite well, it seems, in translating books to the small screen."

Jackie took a deep breath. There was going to be no way out of this one, that much was clear.

"What exactly shall I do, Dr. Westfall? I mean, in light of Graham Grosset's unwillingness to go ahead—"

"That unwillingness shall melt away, my dear. Melt away."

"I'm not so sure—"

"Trust me."

So Westfall had a trick up his sleeve, Jackie reckoned. "If you say so."

"Very good. Now. Grosset must have a copy of the screenplay. I will see that he hands it over to you, and he can take part in its completion, or not—as he sees fit. But he cannot stand in our way."

"No."

"I have assigned Polly Merton to assist you in this project for the time being."

"Oh." *Great,* thought Jackie. She swallowed her dismay. "Thank you so much, Dr. Westfall. That is very thoughtful of you, but I am perfectly—"

"Not at all, my dear Mrs. Walsh, not at all. It is certainly not our intention to burden you in any way with additional chores of a *clerical* nature. We merely wish to tap your *creative* abilities. Miss Merton will be happy to oblige you in any way. I have spoken to her personally on the matter."

Drat, thought Jackie. "That's very kind," she said. This was all she needed—Polly Merton would soon become her sworn enemy for life. It was already difficult enough to get things done in the department, without that woman's cold-shouldered resentment taking the wind out of her sails at every moment.

Westfall gave Jackie a few tips on how he thought Grosset should be handled. Then he prepared to end the conversation, winding up with an oratorical fillip or two from the dead-and-gone greats of Greece and Rome. Long before he finally hung up, Jackie had stopped listening.

As she put the phone down, she stared blankly out the window at the sunny day outdoors.

She had to admit that the idea of working on the screenplay intrigued her. Since her move back to the city and to Rodgers last fall, Jackie hadn't put pen to paper. And she had begun to find that she missed her writing, such as it had been.

Twelve years ago, she had moved with Cooper to Kingswood, a quiet little exurb twenty-three miles from Palmer. Then, the writing projects had been at first a way to fill time, but eventually they had become her lifeline. She had given up her teaching job, at Cooper's insistence, and there hadn't been enough to do around the house; the time had hung heavy on Jackie's hands. She had never felt that she fit in with the garden-clubbing, good-deed-doing ladies of the suburbs. She liked them all well enough, all of the neighbors and friends she had known in Kingswood, but she had chafed at the bit for months until she found her stride. It had been a difficult transition, and a very lonely time.

And then, through Celestine Barger—Philip's ex-wife— Jackie had gotten her first break in writing for television. She had collaborated on a few episodes of *Triumphant Spirit,* an ill-conceived situation comedy about a ghost who wreaked havoc among the living, paying back the little injustices of life through a variety of hilarious hi-jinx from the Other Side. When the show (mercifully) was canceled, Jackie got another break, working with Celestine on *Cop Lady.* This second show was much more up her alley, and Jackie had managed to learn the ropes of teleplay writing in a very short time.

But in the last three years, she hadn't written a thing. Partly, that was because the logistics of going back and forth to Hollywood for script conferences had become impossible. Her husband had been traveling more and more for his business (and, it later emerged, for pleasure as well), and Peter had needed her full attention.

Maybe it was time to try her hand again. After all, in a way this was a golden opportunity. Jackie had enough experience in "The Industry" to know that getting the movie to the screen would mean an agony of rewriting and endless tugs of war. Grosset, too, was sure to be a problem. But still—it was a chance to try something new, and it *was* a prestigious project. Heaven knew her social life was anything but overwhelming.

She wondered, briefly, what Lieutenant Michael McGowan was doing with himself on this picture-perfect Sunday morning.

With a sigh, Jackie got up from the sofa. The newspaper was still scattered about, in a tableau suggesting infinite leisure. She laughed aloud at the thought and began to clean up.

As she piled the papers neatly in the kitchen recycling bin, a headline in the Metropolitan section caught her eye. "Rodgers Coed Found Dead." With a sinking feeling in her stomach, Jackie read on. There was a picture of Danielle Sherman—a passport-style photo, taken, most likely, from her college application.

The item was brief, saying only that the dead woman had been found in the parking lot at the Blue Jay, not far from the campus, and that the police had no comment at this time.

Jackie began to tremble—first her hands, and then her knees. She leaned her back up against the refrigerator for support, and sank down on the floor.

Philip Barger's murder was having repercussions. This much was clear.

Jake wandered idly into the kitchen and gave Jackie a strange look. After a very few moments, his attention roused her; she rose, splashed some cold water on her face, and dialed Michael McGowan.

CHAPTER 13

"I should have called you last night," McGowan apologized. "I just didn't think of it." He had arrived at Jackie's house within ten minutes of her call, and he was now brewing her a cup of tea, while she sat huddled in a sweater at the kitchen table.

"I think I'm glad you didn't," Jackie replied in a small voice. Her dark eyes were shining, and her face was still quite pale, but she was recovering her spirit. "I think I wouldn't have slept a wink."

"You've got protection." McGowan nodded toward Jake, who was now reposing upon the kitchen floor, his head on his front paws, with one eye on the lieutenant. The other eye was shut tight. "Well trained too."

Jackie looked appreciatively at the dog. "Right."

"Where's Peter?" McGowan brought the tea to the table and sat down with Jackie.

"Out with his father."

"Oh."

Jackie realized this statement was a conversation stopper. "They've gone over to Ward Lake, in a boat. To catch some fish."

"Supper."

"I hope not. I hate cleaning fish." Jackie laughed. "I'm not a great one for outdoor pursuits."

"No?" McGowan sipped at his tea and raised an eyebrow.

"I would have figured you for the original Ivory Soap girl. Purity and all that."

"I'm fairly pure, Lieutenant—"

"Please. Michael."

"Michael." Jackie gave him a brief smile, then grew somber again. "I want you to know—I'm convinced that girl knew something. Remember what her roommates said?"

"I do."

"Well?"

"Jackie. Yes—I think you may be right." He looked at her earnestly. "She didn't confide in you?"

Jackie shook her head. "The only thing she said to me was right after Philip was murdered—right after it was announced, that is. We were supposed to have a demonstration in the editing room. You know, a kind of introduction to the technical side of things."

"Right."

"Well of course *that* was canceled. Postponed, I should say. And I asked her—because I knew about her relationship with Philip, you understand—"

"You knew about it before the murder?"

"Sure. Everyone knew. David Surtees even wanted to make a little book on it." Jackie flushed briefly, suddenly conscious that gambling was illegal. McGowan read her thought and chuckled.

"It's okay. I won't arrest him. Tell me about it."

"Oh. Well—you know—would Barger keep her around through finals? Or would it be over before the semester ended? Ha ha." Jackie frowned. "I think David had a thing for Danielle. He may even have been jealous of Barger."

McGowan nodded. "So, did anyone place a bet?"

Jackie concentrated. "No. But I seem to recall that Mark had a funny reaction to the whole thing."

"That would be Mark Freeman?"

"Yes. The animation man."

"What did he say?"

"He tends to be a little sarcastic. In the nicest possible way, of course, and he never means anything by it. Really."

"I follow," replied McGowan. "And?"

"He said, 'Barger won't let her go until he knows what she's got on him.' "

"What did he mean by that?"

"Well, *I* don't know. I assumed he meant something, er, having to do with Barger's romantic history."

"Where did this conversation take place?"

"In the faculty lounge. Over coffee."

"Were other members of the department present?"

"Um, let me see." Jackie took a long sip of her tea and ran her fingers thoughtfully through her dense black curls. "I'm fairly sure Polly Merton was there. She was putting some kind of note in everyone's pigeonhole."

"Anyone else?"

"Let's see. David, Mark, Polly, me. Yes—Yelena Gruber, the acting teacher. She quoted something from Chekhov, and everyone laughed." Jackie frowned at McGowan. "You think that Danielle Sherman *did* have something on Barger?"

"It's a possibility. From what our investigation shows us, he was definitely the kind of guy you could get something on, I think, if you wanted to."

"But why on earth would Danielle Sherman want to?"

McGowan shrugged his shoulders. "Maybe she was a snoopy kind of woman. Some people are like that—prying and poking into other people's affairs all the time."

"Intrusive," said Jackie with a small shudder. Her ex-husband had been that way. She had come home one day to find him rummaging through her desk. She never would have given the episode two minutes thought, if she hadn't seen the guilty look on his face. She had never been able to figure out what he had been searching for, amid all the papers and letters and notes and bills that were heaped high. Until that moment, her life had been an open book for him; afterward, things between them had never been the same.

Which was odd, when you considered that he had been the one with things to hide.

"Jackie? You there?" McGowan wiggled his fingers at her.

"Lost in thought." Jackie smiled. "Okay. So—we start from the premise that Danielle Sherman had something on Barger. Did she blackmail him?"

"And if she did," pursued McGowan, "why is he the one who was killed?"

"Maybe she was blackmailing someone else, who was being blackmailed by Barger," chattered Jackie.

"Whoa, whoa—too many cooks." McGowan shook his head. "Let's try to keep it simple."

"Right." Jackie bit her lower lip gently, a look of thoughtful abstraction crossing her face. "Okay. She wasn't blackmailing him. But she knew something, and so she was dangerous to him."

"If she was dangerous to him, why was he the one killed? It won't work."

"They were both dangerous," Jackie suggested.

"Now we're talking."

"We just have to find out why."

" 'We'?"

"Well—yes." Jackie stuck her chin out. "You need some-one on the inside, who can ask questions of everyone in the department. Right?"

"I—uh—"

"*You* would arouse far too much uneasiness, poking around in there. Whereas *I* have a mandate to poke around. From the president of the university."

She related to him the details of her conversation with B. Crowder Westfall. "It's the perfect cover. I can start out by talking about Barger's screenplay, which would be natural, and from there I can just go on to talk about Barger. Perfect." She grinned brightly at him.

"Jackie, I'm not at all sure—"

"Well, I have to do all this poking anyway. So you might

as well let me report to you. Otherwise you'll never get anywhere. Right?"

"I sure as heck can't stop you." McGowan grinned.

"Right. So, what shall I do first?" she asked eagerly.

"First," said McGowan, pushing back his chair and rising, "you should come with me. We'll have some lunch, and go for a walk."

Jackie looked at her watch. "It's only ten-thirty," she protested.

"Fine. We'll go for a walk, and then have lunch. Okay with you?"

"I have a better idea. You get back to work on the case, and I'll do some research."

"Research?"

"I'm headed to the university bookstore," replied Jackie, pulling on her coat. She took Jake's leash down from its peg, and the dog rose, tail wagging. "It's high time I reread those books, especially if I'm going to be roped into working on this project."

On Monday morning at nine o'clock, Jackie was seated in the faculty lounge in the English department, awaiting the arrival of Graham Grosset. According to the departmental secretary, he had a seminar at nine forty-five, but usually showed up early to keep appointments with students, in a rough semblance of office hours.

She had decided, on Sunday evening, that the best way to go about things would be to get to work on Barger's screenplay. She could talk to other members of the department about Barger, under the pretense of talking about the script. But first, she had to get her hands on it. She was fairly sure that Grosset had it, or at least a copy of it.

Jackie occupied her waiting time with a perusal of the English department's bulletin board. There would be a lecture this afternoon on the "Death of Deconstruction," she noted with a yawn. Someone had put up a desperate-looking notice about missing notes for a doctoral thesis

entitled "Dorothy Wordsworth: Natural Sister." Jackie
yawned again. A third sign invited department members
to submit works for the next issue of *Vice-Versa,* the
university's poetry review. Jackie had never read it. She
confined herself to Kipling, Tennyson, Donne, and Spenser
whenever she felt the urge to read poetry.

Jackie was distracted from her perusal of these interesting
notices by a huge commotion, as Graham Grosset blew in.
He nodded coyly to her, doffed his cape, and peered with
one eye into his pigeonhole.

"No one writes any longer," he complained loudly. "My
compatriots have forgotten all about me—or given me up
for lost in this American intellectual sink. How do, my
dear," he added, turning to face Jackie. "I haven't forgotten
you. Not at all. Quite the opposite, in fact, because I have
been hoping that you could lend me some assistance in a
rather noisome little difficulty that has arisen since we last
had the pleasure of chatting together."

"Oh!" Jackie was not at all sure how to respond. Grosset,
fortunately, never wanted for words.

"The only problem with my asking for your help being,
of course, that I have quite forgotten your *name*. Everything
else about you I remembered with perfect clarity— the luster
of your dark hair, the set of your jaw, the sparkle of your
eyes, and above all the great good sense that you radiate.
So few Americans have any sense at all. Rather shocking,
don't you know. So you stood out in my memory, quite
natural, what? A sensible woman. But as for your name—
well, you *will* forgive me, won't you?" He grinned at her,
and his blue eyes shone with mischief.

"I'm Jackie Walsh," replied Jackie, irritated.

"*That's* it," said Grosset, snapping his fingers and sounding thoroughly gratified. "It is a coincidence, finding you
here in our little lounge this morning. Why they call it a
lounge is beyond me. This place is anything but congenial,
and I would certainly never spend more time than absolutely
necessary in here. Would you?"

"No," agreed Jackie, with a look at the frayed sofas and sprung easy chairs, the stale paper coffee cups and the forlorn bulletin board. "No, I wouldn't."

"But I did so particularly wish to talk to you. Won't you come into my parlor?" Grosset swirled about and marched out the door. Jackie scooped up her book bag and newspaper and hustled after him.

Grosset's little office was a masterpiece of overstatement. Apparently he had brought quite a large number of things with him when he arrived from England. Jackie knew, for starters, that the fine old walnut desk and the glass-fronted bookcases were not standard Rodgers University issue, not even for visiting bigwigs. Moreover, there were calf-bound volumes on every shelf, a large silver inkwell on the desk, and on the wall a large black-and-white aerial photograph of a sunburnt hillside. Tuscany, probably, she thought.

With a proprietary, theatrical gesture, Grosset tossed his cape over a bentwood coat rack. Then he gestured Jackie to one end of a worn chesterfield sofa and took a spot at the other end.

"Now," he said, his eyes full of conspiratorial bonhomie, "here is what I need from you. A full and complete accounting of the events in your department. I must say, all these murders are *most* shocking, and I am not at all comfortable with the fact that my screenplay has not yet been returned to me. I have spoken with Philip Barger's tiresome solicitor, a Mr. Silas Holcombe, who tells me that the university wishes to proceed with the project, even in the face of tragedy. This is so?"

"Yes. Yes, in fact, I—"

"I thought as much. I spent yesterday evening trying desperately to reach that illustrious classicist, Mr. Westfall . . . who, I can assure you, has *no* reputation whatsoever on the other side of the Pond. Be that as it may, he is nonetheless secure in his position of dean of faculty; and to his wishes I must submit. He has *not* returned my telephone calls, which

I consider a most ungentlemanly form of behavior. But then I thought of you, my dear, and my impatience melted away, for I realized that in some way I should manage to find you."

"I—"

Grosset held up a hand. "And to tell you once more that the project is simply not on. There." He sat back and smirked at Jackie.

"But, Dr. Grosset—what about your film contract with the university?"

"Pish-tosh. We'll just ignore it, all of us, and go merrily on our way as though nothing at all had happened between us, except of course this *most* felicitous professional arrangement—I mean, my visiting professorship. Because, my dear—just between us—the pay is simply stupendous. *Twice* what one is paid at home. And for that reason, I shall consider extending my term for another year. But not unless there are promises made. The film project is not on." Grosset seemed to have run out of gas at last. He folded his hands primly in his lap and gave Jackie an utterly charming smile.

Jackie took the bull by the horns. She was heartily tired of these windbags pushing her about, telling her that she must do this or that to satisfy them.

"That won't work, I'm afraid. I came to see you this morning to ask your cooperation in going ahead with the project. There are many very good reasons for doing so, I suppose, but the most compelling one is money. There is a large endowment from Stuart Goodwillie riding on this whole business. In order to be certain the university receives the endowment, we must turn over a completed screenplay to the production company."

"I don't understand why," complained Grosset.

"I can't say it pleases me any more than it does you," Jackie added, feeling a blush spread across her face, "but there we are. If the screenplay needs additional work, the dean of faculty has asked me to take up the project. I have no choice but to do it."

"Ah." Grosset lifted an eyebrow. "And are you a writer, as well as a persuader, my dear?"

Jackie hurriedly rummaged in her book bag and pulled out a piece of paper. "I've brought you my CV, so that you can see that I do have some experience in this area. We can turn the script over to Goodwillie Enterprises now, as it stands, or we can work together to improve it."

Grosset took the resumé from her in silence. He read quietly, tut-tutting over a few of the items. "Good heavens!" he exclaimed at last. "*Triumphant Spirit* was a simply dreadful program."

"I know," replied Jackie.

"It was too awful even for ITV, who carried it briefly." He shook his head. "You should take that one off your record, my dear. You really should."

But a change had suddenly come over Grosset. He gave up his pattering protest and was silent for a few moments. At long last, he let out an enormous sigh.

"Well. If we must, we must." He rose and went to a large oak filing cabinet that was fitted with a singularly impressive padlock. "What is it you say over here? 'You mustn't fight City Hall,' isn't that it? So quaint, you Yanks." He opened the top drawer, groped about, and finally pulled out a thick manila folder.

He handed the folder over to Jackie. "Here you go. This is Philip Barger's last draft. It's not complete—only takes us up through chapter fifteen, where the hunchbacked friar tries to kill the nun. And it's perfectly dreadful. Really awful."

Jackie opened the folder with great curiosity and leafed quickly through the first few pages. The dialogue, she felt, certainly left something to be desired. But then again, so did the dialogue in Grosset's books, which was always full of mysterious references that Jackie had to stop and look up.

Grosset seemed to have recovered his spirits, for he began again to prattle away at Jackie. She listened, distracted, to a long description of how little Barger had appreciated the Kestrel books, and how unsuited he had been, in fact, to write a screenplay.

"The man's mind was indelicate, his learning was spotty, and his ear was of tin. I don't see how he ever got the urge to write, in fact—he was so obviously unsuited to the task. And he hated to work. I had the most awful time persuading him to rewrite anything."

"Because he was stubborn?"

"My dearest child, *no*. Because he was lazy. He was the laziest person I have ever known—and my own country, you know, is full of all kinds of people who make a career of just lying about. Most of them get knighted for it." His face took on a wistful look. "I had rather been hoping for a K.B.E. myself, but I'm afraid I've been far too industrious. So far, Her Majesty has taken very little note of me. Ah, well." He brightened again. "There's nothing at all wrong with lassitude, if you can still pay the rates. But Barger pretended *not* to be lazy, when he was. Unforgivable."

"Hmm," said Jackie. She had always thought it strange that Barger should be interested in tackling such a grand project. "You have no idea why he wanted to undertake it?"

"Well, the *money*, of course. Same reason I agreed to it—the money was going to be fabulous."

"Yes, I suppose so."

"But, speaking quite frankly, my dear, I'd have thought he'd have been far better off writing a movie called *Swedish Au Pairs*, or something like that."

"Yes," agreed Jackie quietly.

"I hope I don't shock you?"

Jackie frowned. "Dr. Grosset—if this is Barger's last draft, how did you get hold of it? The police have been searching for it left and right, and even Barger's secretary couldn't find it."

"Well, my dear, that's just going to be my little secret. But you have it now. I have done what you asked." He looked at her sternly. "Now that we have had this little chat, I feel ever so much better. It seems to me that my reputation may be saved, after all. My advice to you," he said, wagging a finger at the folder in Jackie's lap, "is to chuck it."

"We can't." Jackie wondered again why Grosset had stopped writing. Maybe he was still writing, but not producing anything worthy—hence the need for the film contract and the visiting professorship. She was on the point of asking him, but something in his eyes stopped her. There would be time enough for that sort of question later, if they got this project off the ground.

"Well, then," said Grosset airily, "perhaps we shall be able to salvage something of this miserable enterprise." He pulled a gold watch from his pocket, glanced at it, and rose. "If you will forgive me, we must end this interview. I shall expect to hear from you. But just now there is a nasty gaggle of teenagers awaiting me in Room 312."

CHAPTER 14

Back in her own office at the Longacre Center, Jackie read quickly through the materials in the folder. It had been ten years, at least, since she had last read the Kestrel books; even so, she could tell at a glance that Barger's script had fallen well short of the mark. Small wonder that Grosset had wanted to call the whole thing off.

Jackie picked up the copy of the novel, which she had bought on Sunday afternoon, and began to skim through it, comparing the story to the drama as written. She broke off this absorbing activity long enough to take her three o'clock lecture class; and she continued her reading that night, long after Peter had gone to bed, taking Jake upstairs with him.

By the next morning, Jackie was convinced that the script, as written, was useless. She called and spoke to Grosset, but his mood of airy insouciance left her feeling helpless once more. The illustrious author was determined to be uncooperative, in the most charming way possible, but Jackie (to her own surprise) was likewise determined that this project should reach a conclusion, one way or another.

She needed advice. Jackie reached once more for the telephone and called her friend in the English department, Millicent Brooks, explained the situation to her, and arranged for the two of them to have lunch.

"So what's the scoop?" asked Millicent as they settled down over tuna-fish sandwiches in the cafeteria.

"The scoop is, I don't get it. We've got a reluctant author who stands to make about a million dollars, only he won't cooperate. We've got a dead professor, who wrote badly and should never, by rights, have been allowed near that work. I finally get my hands on this famous script, only to find out that there are huge chunks of the story missing."

"Last point first," said Millicent, who had an organized mind. "Aren't screenplays always like that?"

"Usually," Jackie agreed, "but there is something fishy about this. Have you read Grosset?"

"Of course. He's *required*." Millicent chuckled. "But I hate the way he writes. His style is like a cross between Henry James, Henry Miller, and Judith Krantz."

Jackie laughed. Millicent had a point. "Well, listen. Whether you hate him or not—it's weird. This story really doesn't seem to have much to do with the books at all. It's truly terrible."

"Great! So you can just rewrite it, become rich and famous, and win an Oscar."

"Why stop there?" responded Jackie with a laugh. "Why not the Pulitzer, or the Nobel Prize for Screenplays?" The two friends giggled. "But seriously. There is a whole lot missing."

"Talk to Grosset about it."

"I did," replied Jackie. "I called him this morning. He told me that the book had really been just a 'product of his misspent youth,' and that the character of the schoolmaster wasn't that important."

"Wait a second. The *schoolmaster* is missing?"

"Right." Jackie nodded. "See, I told you it was weird."

"But the schoolmaster is the one who solves the whole puzzle in Book Three."

"Right."

"That *is* bizarre."

"There's more. Listen. I thought Barger was the one who had made the change. So I suggested to Grosset that we should put the schoolmaster back in, but he said no."

"Huh?"

"Now—how can you make a movie of the Kestrel books without the schoolmaster?"

"You can't."

"Right." Jackie took a huge bite of her sandwich and chewed thoughtfully.

"So what are you going to do?"

"The whole thing seems crazy to me. It seems like Grosset is just determined to make my job difficult. I think I'll talk to Dr. Westfall again today, and explain the situation to him. With any luck, we can let Stuart Goodwillie *think* we're going ahead with it, and he'll come up with the endowment money, and then we can all ignore the whole thing."

"Don't you want to get rich and famous?"

"Not if I have to collaborate with an author who has removed the most important character from his own story. Too much of a hassle."

"I see what you mean. Oh, I talked to John's student the other day—she and her husband came by for dinner, and of course we couldn't talk *frankly* about her past whatever-it-was—I guess you'd call it a *liaison*—with Barger. Not with her husband sitting right there. But I finally got her into the kitchen to help with the dishes. She says Polly Merton used to keep all of Barger's files. Every one. Even his alimony payments folder."

"Hmm." Jackie digested this fact. She was momentarily surprised that Celestine Barger had accepted any form of support from her ex-husband; issues of independence and pride aside, Celestine Barger was a very wealthy woman in her own right. But upon consideration of the sleaze factor, Jackie supposed she had been justified. It may have gratified her to make Barger squirm once a month. "I wonder why Polly didn't have the Kestrel script," said Jackie at last.

"I wonder. Maybe you should ask your handsome policeman." Millicent looked at her friend intently, and the conversation strayed, quite naturally, to the topic of Lieutenant Michael McGowan, and his many virtues.

• • •

"Asphyxiation," said Cosmo Gordon to Michael Mc-Gowan. They were seated in McGowan's little cubicle, drinking bad coffee and going over the postmortem report on Danielle Sherman. "That girl was murdered. The autopsy showed that the heroin hadn't even reached her heart."

"You mean she was injected with the stuff after she was killed."

"You got it."

"What else?"

"Seems to have been knocked out, with some sort of heavy instrument, and then suffocated. The lab found traces of some kind of fabric, which they analyzed. Turns out to be cashmere, very expensive stuff."

"A sweater?"

Gordon shook his head. "They can't really tell, but it looks like a thick weave. A blanket, or a coat. Thin, fine threads. Not knitted."

"Great. So we arrest everyone in Palmer with a cashmere coat."

"That would be a start."

"Swell. *You* arrest them." McGowan rubbed his chin thoughtfully. "I've talked to several witnesses, people who were at the Blue Jay on Thursday and Friday nights. Nobody admits to having seen anyone dumping a body."

"Yeah. The Blue Jay crowd make such great witnesses too. It's just as well—a jury would never go for it. No, Mike. If you don't mind a little fatherly advice—"

"Mind? That's why you're here. I'll buy you a beer, later."

"You're on. All right, then. You're going to have to go about this one another way. From the other direction."

"I know." McGowan shoved a thick manila folder across the desk. "Here's the roundup for the Barger murder. Anybody could have doctored that drink, but somebody had to be at the department to get the key, open the door, and drag the body into that room."

"Which means sometime between nine and midnight. The lab report indicates that the body wasn't moved after rigor had set in. Tell me what you've got."

McGowan took a breath. "Unfortunately, the usual suspects are out. The ex-wife has an alibi for the whole of that night—she was staying overnight with a friend."

"They swear she was there all night?"

"Yeah." McGowan chuckled. "They swear."

"Okay." Gordon thumbed through the file. "And the other usual suspects?"

"The girlfriend, of course. Except she wound up dead. So I would say that lets her out of the running."

"You could say that. What about this guy"—Gordon tapped at the folder—"Freeman?"

"We can't rule him out. But so far, I can't find a reason why he'd want to kill Barger. They weren't friends, but Barger worked hard to keep on the right side of him. He was a big draw for the department, for students and for grant money. Half of their new equipment came in on his account."

"The goose that laid the golden eggs."

"More or less. He has no alibi, but I don't see it. Now, the English guy—the writer, Grosset. He's an interesting one."

"Why?"

"He's what you call an eccentric genius. Goes around dressed in a cape. Barger was working on a screenplay from his books, so we know there was a connection."

"The Kestrel books?"

"That's right."

"He is a weirdo." Gordon read the profile on Graham Grosset with interest. "Never wrote anything more?"

McGowan shook his head. "Nope. One of those early burnouts, maybe—you know, big success, followed by thirty years of stubborn hermitlike existence, refusing all interviews."

"Except he's here, right out in the open."

"Yup. First time in twenty years that he's been out in the open. According to my source, Grosset wasn't pleased with the way the film was taking shape. I—er—I'm waiting to hear further information on him."

"Oh?" Gordon was interested.

"Yes, well, my friend in the department—"

"Oh, ho!"

"Knock it off." McGowan grinned. "She's been assigned to try to figure out where the film project stands. By Henry Obermaier."

"Top brass," said Gordon, his voice heavy with irony. "Why?"

"Because of some money that crank Goodwillie says he wants to give the university. All politics. But Jackie's doing a little digging into Grosset's past for me."

"Naturally, you'll have to take her out to dinner on the department to find out what she's discovered."

"Maybe I'll cook her a hot dog at my place," McGowan retorted.

Gordon flipped through the files. "Merida Green. She's the new department head. What have you got on her?"

"A regular grouch from dawn till dusk, as far as I can tell. But she was up in Boston the night that Barger was killed, at a meeting of some sort. She gave a speech, plenty of witnesses."

"Too bad. What time was the speech?"

"Six o'clock. There was a cocktail reception afterward, a hundred and fifty women from film departments all around the Northeast."

"A wild night, no doubt," smirked Gordon. He flipped the pages of the folder again. "What's this mean—'Like a nun'?"

"She's a weirdo, the department secretary. Polly Merton. She dresses all in black, or all in white, or all in black and white. Long, straight hair, skinny, steel glasses on her nose, and butter wouldn't melt in her mouth."

"If I were given to generalization, which I'm not, I'd say she's a good type for a poisoner."

"That's what I thought. And she certainly had opportunity. She was the only one with the spare key to the room where Barger's body was found; and her office has a door leading into his. Plus she probably knew when he would be working late, and she could have doctored that liqueur at any time, then just sat back and waited. She seems like the type who's good at waiting."

"But what kind of motive would she have?"

"Who knows? Maybe I should get her back in here, do a little more digging."

"Did she know the Sherman girl?"

"I don't think so. Danielle Sherman was only taking one course at the Longacre Center."

"Then how did Barger get his hands on her so fast?"

"I think he just spotted her one day. He moved fast, as far as we can tell. That was his M.O."

"Class act, that guy."

"Top drawer," agreed McGowan.

Gordon flipped the page. "How about this other instructor, Surtees. He was the one who was with your friend when the body was found?"

"I think we can pretty much rule him out. He was out that night at a dinner party—although there seems to be some evidence that he was sweet on the Sherman girl."

"What kind of evidence?"

"Did I say evidence? Sorry, hearsay. Not evidence. It probably doesn't amount to anything, anyway."

"Okay. Did you check his alibi?"

"Sure. It checks out."

Gordon yawned. "Mike, you don't have anything."

"Don't I know it." McGowan ran his hands through his hair. "The only angle I could figure was some mistress or other doing a slow burn. But the ones I talked to didn't check out. Only one still in town, and she's happily married, getting her Ph.D. in the physics department."

Gordon shook his head. "That's no guarantee, Mike. Nancy and I have been happily married for twenty-four years, and I'm still jealous of her college sweetheart."

"Not really?"

"Sure." Gordon inched up his shoulders and smiled. "She loved him. She probably still loves him, deep down, in some way that she'll never love me. That's reason enough."

McGowan shook his head. Gordon had a sentimental streak, no doubt about it. "Yeah—but from what I can tell, Mary Richmond never loved Barger."

"Oh. Well, I suppose that makes it different. But I don't understand that kind of thing. Never will."

"Then you're one of the lucky ones."

CHAPTER 15

On Monday night, Jackie Walsh brooded. There was something that she knew—only, like Danielle Sherman, she didn't know she knew.

The thought of Danielle Sherman distressed Jackie even further. McGowan had told her that Danielle's death was being ruled a homicide. The drugs that had caused the apparent overdose had been injected into her system after her heart had stopped; the cause of death was asphyxiation.

Jackie owed this much knowledge to McGowan, who had called her that afternoon with a report. She had studiously avoided reading the newspaper accounts of the young woman's death; she was trying to escape the notion that there might have been a way for her to prevent it. By late Monday night, the notion had become a certainty in her mind.

Jackie knew this conviction to be unreasonable and unfounded, but like many people, she felt a responsibility for events and circumstances beyond her influence. Besides— Jackie hadn't liked Danielle. She had, in fact, disliked her— had considered her arrogant, selfish, and rather stupid. The awareness of this antipathy only served to intensify the guilt that she felt.

Peter had gone to bed, taking Jake with him; at midnight, still sleepless, Jackie tiptoed into her son's bedroom and roused the sleeping dog.

"You come with me, fella," she whispered. Jake cocked
an eye at her, yawned, and followed.

Jackie and Jake settled themselves downstairs in the back
sitting room, Jackie under a blanket on the sofa, with a cup
of tea at her elbow, and Jake snoring contentedly on the
floor beside her. She reached for the TV remote control
and flipped idly through the channels, finally settling on
The Lady From Shanghai—for perhaps the thirtieth time
in her life.

But Welles's ironic tale of treachery and murder plans
gone awry did nothing to soothe her mind, and before
long she found herself changing the channels again, almost
manically. In just this way, Cooper Walsh had flipped
through the channels, driving her crazy. It was a habit that
Jackie, for no good reason, considered to be particularly
male, and particularly annoying.

When she had had enough of the automobile commercials, and dating-service commercials, and the men's hair-
weave commercials, she flipped off the television. The
silence that followed was huge. Jake stirred. Jackie reached
down and scratched his head gently.

Then, with no warning, Jake was up, on his feet, barking and snarling with a fury that seemed almost unreal to
Jackie. He made a dash for the front door and hurled himself
against it; the force of his drive repelled him to the floor,
but in a split second he was up again, savagely throwing
himself at the door, clawing at the wood with frenzy, baring
his teeth.

Jackie, her heart pounding, felt time slow to a standstill.
A cold panic seized her. This was what she had been
dreading—this dog had lost his grip, and was turning on
them with a ferocity that was truly terrifying. She took a
careful, slow step backward. Why in heaven's name had
she allowed this terrible animal into their house? She moved
silently, and as smoothly as her frayed nerves would permit,
groping against the wall for support. She finally reached
the staircase, just as Jake turned. The ferocity in his eyes

chilled her to the bone; he seemed to look right through her, with no sign of recognition. Running now entirely on adrenaline, Jackie tore up the stairs and fled into Peter's room, slamming the door behind her.

"Mom? What's the matter with Jake?" asked Peter. His cheeks and lips were puffy with sleep, and his thick reddish hair stood away from his face in a curious rooster-tail effect. Jackie felt her eyes well with tears as she moved, with panicky steps, toward Peter's small dresser. With clumsy movements she shoved it in front of the door, and felt the hot tears coursing down her face.

"Mom?" Peter turned on the lamp at his bedside.

"Hush, baby. It's okay." Her voice shook.

"Mom, what's Jake barking at? What's the matter?"

Jackie dragged a chair and placed it carefully in front of the dresser, forcing the back of the chair up under the wooden drawer-pulls.

"Mom? What are you doing? Mom?"

"Hush, baby," said Jackie again. By this time Peter was wide awake. He listened to the sounds coming from downstairs—Jake's low, throaty growl, followed by deep, menacing barks.

"Jake's barking at someone in the kitchen," said Peter. "Who's in the kitchen with Jake?"

Jackie stopped trembling long enough to orient herself to the sound. Peter was right. Jake was now below them, in the kitchen. She could hear the frenzy with which he hurled himself violently against the back door, all the while keeping up his savage barking.

Maybe the dog hadn't, after all, lost his mind.

"Turn out the light, Peter."

"But, Mom—"

"Turn out the light. Now."

Peter obeyed. Jackie went slowly to the window at the back of Peter's room and looked out. The small backyard was in darkness, but the alley beyond was illuminated by

a pool of muddy yellow light from a street lamp near the
corner. Jackie stood well back from the window and held
her breath. A dim figure was moving swiftly through the
shadows in the yard. Now it opened the gate and stepped
out into the alley. Jackie caught a glimpse of a dark jacket
and dark trousers; the person wore a hat, and the face was
in shadow.

A shiver ran through her. Peter had joined her, and stood
watching in silence.

"Who is that, Mom?" he asked finally.

"I don't know, sweetie." She ruffled his hair. As the panic
left her, Jackie's palms grew clammy, and she started to
shake once more. "I don't know."

The house was quiet again. Jackie listened carefully; she
could hear Jake padding across the downstairs hall, his
toenails clip-clipping across the bare wooden floor.

Peter looked up at his mother. "Jake did a pretty good
job, didn't he, Mom?"

"He sure did, Petey. He sure did."

"Height?" asked the young policewoman seated at the
kitchen table with Jackie.

When her terror had finally subsided, Jackie had called
the police, and after about thirty minutes two officers had
appeared to take her statement. One, a young man, was outside searching the area, but Jackie was certain the intruder
was by now long gone.

"I don't know. Maybe about five-ten, or so."

"And you don't know if it was a man or a woman?"
The young woman's tone indicated that she thought this
midnight alarm was a waste of taxpayer money. The Palmer
police had better things to do than to comfort a frightened
woman.

"The yard is dark, as you'll no doubt have noticed,"
remarked Jackie. "And the alley light doesn't do a whole
lot." Jackie was feeling self-conscious and silly. "Listen,
um, Officer."

"Yes?"

"Ordinarily I would never have called you—I mean, we live in the city, Peter and I, and we are prepared to deal with the risks of being here. But I'm afraid my nerves are a little frayed, on account of the murders at the university."

Jackie could tell that this explanation cut little ice. The policewoman merely nodded, so Jackie went on. "They were people I knew," she said quietly.

"I see." The policewoman regarded Jackie with greater care. "Has anyone talked to you about those murders?"

"Oh, yes. Yes. Lieutenant McGowan and I have had several conversations."

Jackie detected a slight shift in the other woman's manner. Discomfiture? Interest? It was impossible to say.

"Perhaps I should call him now," suggested the policewoman.

"Oh, no—I wouldn't bother him." Jackie glanced up at the big clock on the wall over the sink. "It's nearly two-thirty."

"Do you have any reason to think, Mrs. Walsh, that your intruder was not an ordinary burglar?"

"No—no. I really don't."

"But you're not certain."

"Well—the thing is that our dog Jake was barking up a storm." She stretched a foot out under the kitchen table and rested it on Jake's back. The fur felt warm and thick, and Jake's back rose and fell with his regular breathing. Jackie was comforted. "If I were a burglar, and I heard that bark, I wouldn't bother to go around the house to the back door. If you follow me. I would be warned off."

"But this person was persistent?"

"I think so. Jake heard him out front, and then out back."

"Did you follow the dog? To the kitchen door?"

"I—um, no. I went upstairs. I was terrified." A sudden wave of guilt washed over Jackie. How could she have doubted their wonderful dog? Too many Stephen King movies, she supposed. Next, she'd probably suspect their Jeep of harboring evil thoughts. "I went upstairs into Peter's bedroom—my son's bedroom."

"Is there a telephone in there?"

"No."

"The next time something like this happens, Mrs. Walsh, I suggest you hide out in a room with a telephone. In case you need to call for help."

"I just wasn't thinking. I panicked." Jackie had to admit that she hadn't stood this test very well. She hoped to heaven that there wouldn't be a next time, but she had to admit the advice was sound.

"I'll file a report. There's really nothing that we can do, you know, unless we can demonstrate that a crime of some sort was committed. There isn't really a law against someone approaching your door, even at midnight."

"No," agreed Jackie.

The woman stood to go as her partner reappeared through the kitchen door. "Nothing," he said with barely a look at Jackie.

"Thank you very much for coming," said Jackie. She meant her thanks, but the visit hadn't done anything to calm her fears.

When they had gone, Jackie checked on Peter. He was sleeping deeply. It was at least another hour before she dropped off to sleep, thankful for Jake.

The next morning, Jackie found herself in Polly Merton's office, being scolded.

"I really don't have time for this, you know," insisted Polly, adjusting the skirt of her muslin dress and folding her neat little hands on her desk. "I am responsible for the needs of an entire department, and I don't really see why I should put off doing things for others just to—"

"Wait, wait. Polly, please." Jackie Walsh had a headache. After the events of the previous night, it wasn't surprising. She was in no mood for Polly Merton, with her perfect notions of how things should be done, and her eager, repressed energy. "Polly, I wish you wouldn't get the wrong idea about all of this. It's just that Dr. Westfall has left me little choice in the matter. I don't think I'll really need much in the way of assistance, at all. But I did want to talk to you about the project."

"Talk away," said Polly, a small smile crossing her thin, pale lips. "Maybe that will make you feel better. But I have nothing to contribute. And we're so busy right now that I can't possibly schedule any typing time for you."

"I don't need you to type. I can do my own typing— always have, always will." Jackie smiled brightly, but her attempt at a display of good humor was wasted, as it usually was on Polly. Polly Merton merely stared at her, her blue eyes alight with incomprehension and nervousness. "Okay, Polly. All I really want to know is if you have any kind of notes—dictation or research notes—that Philip might have left behind."

"Nothing about Graham Grosset. The rest of his papers belong to the department, Jackie. You'll have to clear it with Ms. Green if you want to access them."

Jackie bridled. She hated the word "access" when used as a verb. It had been one of her husband's words, irritating in a small way for a dozen years. The reminder of that irritation made Jackie more tenacious. "I think that Dr. Westfall has spoken to you about all of this, Polly. I am only doing what he asked—and frankly, I see no reason why you shouldn't cooperate with his request as well."

"I have cooperated. He didn't ask me to give you the run of the department files."

"No. Just Philip Barger's files. I promise not to take anything away—will that make you feel better?"

"You can't work in here." Polly looked around her spare little office, which was neat as a pin, as always. Everything was in perfect order: All the file folders upright, neatly marked, and precisely aligned. The very pens and pencils in the white cup on the desk seemed to stand more erect under Polly Merton's unforgiving stare. A single white gardenia blossom floated in a small china bowl on the windowsill. Polly always had a discreet flower or two in her office—a habit that surprised Jackie. It seemed so unlike the woman. But she supposed even the Polly Mertons of this world knew how to appreciate flowers.

"I wouldn't dream of it. I'll tell you what." She reached in her bag and pulled out a yellow legal pad. "Let's make a list of everything that I take to my office. Then you can check it all off as I return it. Okay?"

Polly Merton, faced with this suggestion, had to back down. She agreed to Jackie's terms, with a stipulation that everything was to be back in its place by the end of the week. Then the two women set about removing Philip Barger's file folders from the little accessory room off Polly's office. This process took nearly an hour, because Polly insisted on making the list of the files' contents herself, writing slowly and methodically, giving each folder a name and a label, and then copying it all laboriously onto her own yellow pad. When this important work was at last accomplished, Jackie retreated to her own tiny office and set to work browsing through them.

She had been at the task for less than half an hour when the telephone rang. It was Merida Green.

"Jackie, I wanted to remind you of the promise you made to me last week."

Oh, damn, thought Jackie in a panic. It was Tuesday. The midterm grades were due at the registrar's office by five o'clock, and Jackie wasn't finished marking the papers. "Yes, Merida. I haven't forgotten." Jackie looked at her watch: eleven-fifteen. She had a two o'clock class, but she might just be able to finish grading the papers if she hustled.

"Jackie?"

"Yes, Merida?"

"Have you finished with those papers?"

"Just finishing up right now, Merida," Jackie lied. "Then I want to make a few notes for myself, finish writing comments, and of course ask Polly to make those copies you wanted."

"On my desk by four," said Merida. "I won't be here any later than that today." She hung up.

Muttering, Jackie moved Barger's notes to her windowsill and reached for the stack of midterm papers. There were four left to read through, including Danielle Sherman's, which had been buried in a pile of correspondence that Jackie had retrieved yesterday from her pigeonhole.

For just a moment, Jackie caught herself thinking that the paper hadn't been the reason that Danielle didn't turn up in class that day. Jackie shook her head. What a crazy thing to think! Of course Danielle hadn't skipped class; she had been dead by Friday morning, according to the police. Jackie had simply become confused for a second—these murders were making her crazy, no question.

Jackie shook her head, then looked with curiosity at the dead student's paper. It had been neatly typed, with her name and the date on the cover page. Jackie was tempted to read it; but with a grim sense of pragmatism, she put the paper aside and quickly made her way through the other three essays. Then she wrote up her midterm report, gathered up the papers for Polly to photocopy, and headed off for the registrar's office.

When she returned to the Longacre Center, it was exactly two o'clock. Jackie had canceled yesterday's class, as a gesture for Danielle. Today, she greeted a somber and uncomfortable-looking bunch. They engaged in a desultory conversation about a Kurosawa film that someone had seen the night before. But none of them had any heart for film today. Jackie dismissed them, but was grateful when Nadia Pitts stayed to talk, briefly. There wasn't, in truth, much that either one of them could say, but it comforted Jackie to talk to the student who had been Danielle's friend.

"The police don't seem to know anything," Nadia complained. "They won't even talk to me about how she died. I know it wasn't a drug overdose—obviously. Right?"

"I bet you are right," agreed Jackie, sounding as noncommittal as she could. "Nadia—did Danielle give you any idea of who it might have been that she went to meet on Thursday?"

"No. I think she usually spent Thursday nights with Philip. And even though they had kind of broken up before he—before he died, I figured that maybe she was missing him. You know how even when it's right to break up you sometimes still miss the person."

"That's for sure," replied Jackie.

"So I thought maybe she had gone over to one of the frat houses for a party or something. They have keg parties on Thursday nights at the Castle." The Castle was one of the truly notorious fraternities at Rodgers University, and the Castle's Thursday night keg parties were a thorn in the administration's side. But no amount of threatening or bribery seemed to persuade the students to give up their rowdy ways. Jackie knew all about Thursday nights at the Castle.

"But Danielle didn't turn up there?"

"Nope. Nobody knows where she went."

"Somebody will find out."

"Yeah. Someday." Nadia Pitts picked up her bag and headed out the door. Jackie followed suit.

When she returned to her office, Jackie knew at once that something was wrong. She glanced about, but couldn't put her finger on it. Yet all of her books and papers seemed to be in order—and heaven knew there was nothing else in the office to interest even the most dimwitted of thieves. She saw with relief that Philip Barger's notes were still on the windowsill; she thumbed through them quickly. All present and accounted for. She would have hated to have to tell Polly Merton that something was lost.

Jackie shrugged her shoulders and sat down behind her desk. Then she realized—Danielle Sherman's midterm paper wasn't there. Had she taken it to Polly, with the others, to be photocopied? No. Definitely not. Crazy and tired and stressed out as she was, Jackie knew for certain that she had left Danielle's midterm on the corner of her desk.

CHAPTER 16

"Hey, there."

Jackie looked up. Mark Freeman was standing in her doorway. He had stolen up on her very quietly. "Everything okay, Jackie? You look like you've seen a ghost."

"Oh, Mark. God, what an awful day. Awful week."

"What's the matter?"

"Nerves. Shattered." Jackie, on the verge of telling Mark Freeman about the missing paper, clammed up. "But other than that, nothing. Nothing at all."

"I thought maybe I could pry you loose for a beer down at the Juniper."

"Oh." Jackie looked at her watch. Where had the day gone? It was nearly four-thirty. She thought for a moment. Peter was spending the afternoon and early evening with his friend Bobby. "Sure. Just let me put a few things away. I'll meet you in the lobby in ten minutes, all right?"

"Perfect." Mark departed, and Jackie tidied up. Mindful of her solemn promise to Polly Merton not to take the Barger notes anywhere, she carefully tucked the pile of folders into her book bag. Jackie Walsh was not above grabbing a little private revenge, if it didn't hurt anyone.

There was quite a crowd at the Juniper, but Jackie and Mark managed to find themselves a quiet table in the far back corner. They settled in with their beers, and Jackie felt herself begin to relax. It felt like years since she had last relaxed.

"I hear Merida's down on you, Jackie," said Mark with a smile.

"That's not news," replied Jackie with a grin. "She's always hated me."

"Well, she hates you even worse now. Does that bother you?"

"Of course. I don't like anyone to hate me, especially when it's just personal, but they make it professional. If you know what I mean."

"Do I ever. You're not alone. She hates us all."

"She hated Philip the most."

"The most of everyone who hated Philip, or the most of the people she hates?" Mark smiled, and his brown eyes shone.

He really has a cool streak in him, thought Jackie. "Both. I think."

"Have you seen Celestine?"

Jackie shook her head. "I wrote her a note, of course. It's awkward, because they've been divorced for so long. Still, Philip's death had to be a shock for her."

"Of course. In a way, it might be harder."

"No. In some cases, maybe. But not for Celestine. Not where Philip is concerned."

"No, I suppose you're right. By the way, I went to see Merida, to ask her to authorize payment for the new computer. I went on bended knee. I went with hat in hand."

Jackie laughed. "What did she say?"

"That Philip must have had his reasons for reneging on the purchase of my computer, and that his reasons were good enough for her, and that she was only chairperson pro tem, and couldn't be responsible for making major decisions, and so forth. She passed the buck, in other words, pretty effectively."

"Thank heavens it's only pro tem," replied Jackie.

"Right. When they make Polly Merton the department

head, I'll stand a better chance." He nodded solemnly. "But in the meantime, Jackie, I feel guilty. I ducked the police when they talked to me the first time, but I think they think I had a motive. And now it's too late to tell that detective the truth—that I did have an argument with Philip. So you have to help me invent a really good lie. One that will work."

Jackie shook her head. "Mark, just tell McGowan the truth."

"Tell McGowan the truth about what?" said a voice.

"Uh-oh," said Mark, his face falling with comic rapidity. "You caught me. Jackie—did you set me up?"

Jackie wheeled around. Michael McGowan was standing behind her, a beer in one hand and a bag of peanuts in the other.

"Hi, Lieutenant," said Jackie, feeling awkward. "I believe you know my colleague, Mark Freeman?"

"We've met," said McGowan. "The truth about what?"

Mark sighed deeply, a look of contrition on his face. "I lied, Lieutenant. But I am now prepared to make a clean breast of things, to apologize fully, and to offer you justification for my behavior."

McGowan passed the peanuts around. "Don't sweat it," he said. "If you mean the little dust-up you had with Barger about your computer. We got it all from the secretary. Miss Manners."

"No!" Jackie and Mark looked at each other and burst out laughing. "The departmental spokeswoman," said Mark, chuckling.

"She sure as shootin' has you all pegged," concurred McGowan. "There isn't anything that she doesn't know about."

"Then how come she doesn't know who killed Philip? And Danielle Sherman, for that matter?" Mark sounded genuinely incensed.

"Maybe she does," said Jackie. "Maybe she's just not telling."

Mark Freeman drained his beer mug and stood up. "Jackie, I'm off. You coming?"

"No—Jackie's staying," said McGowan. "I need to ask her one or two little questions."

"Ah. You want me to call you a lawyer, Jackie?"

"No, thank you, Mark. If he gets out the tape recorder, then we can call a lawyer."

"Right. Well. See you." He trotted off merrily, leaving Jackie face-to-face with Michael McGowan.

"I've got a little bone to pick with you, Jackie."

"What's that?"

"How come you didn't call me last night when someone tried to break into your house?"

"Oh." Jackie looked steadily at him. "I dialed 911."

"Right. But listen—get this straight. Two points. First of all, there is a murderer on the loose. So far, we've got zip, zero, zilch on this guy. Motive is especially cloudy; could even be a random series. And so that means that every member of your department could be in danger."

"No, not really—"

"Point two: I am your policeman. If you need a policeman, I am the one you call. I don't want just any dumb old rookie looking after you and Peter. All right?"

Jackie swallowed hard. "All right," she said at last.

"Good. Now, from the beginning. I want the whole story about last night. Start to finish."

Jackie obliged. "It wasn't just an ordinary burglar, I don't think," she said at last. "I mean—I felt like we'd been singled out."

"I think you're right about that. Where's Peter?"

"He's playing at a friend's house."

"Come on." Without another word, McGowan led the way out of the bar. They climbed into his car, and he followed Jackie's directions to Bobby Blue's house, where they picked up Peter and headed home.

By the time they were all in Jackie's kitchen, and Jake had been fed and walked and talked to, and Jackie had supper on the stove, she was angry. She didn't like the way this man was bossing her around. It was one thing for him to be concerned for her safety; it was quite another for him to tell her how to chop an onion. She finally gave him a look.

"What? I should back off, right?"

"Yes," said Jackie.

"Sorry." McGowan smiled. "Bad habit, telling people how to chop onions."

"Right."

"Okay. So I'll sit here"—he pulled out a chair from the table and sat—"and you can tell me about yourself."

"I'd rather we just talked about the case."

"Okay," said McGowan. "The case. Did you come across any clues today?"

"No."

"Neither did I. So—tell me about yourself."

Jackie, tired of the tug of war, obliged. She was smart enough to realize that the real conflict was in her own mind. She decided, as she made omelettes for the three of them, that she *would* tell McGowan about herself, but that it wouldn't mean anything. It would be just for practice. Because someday—maybe in a year, or six years—she might be ready to really open up to a man again. It might even be this man. Who knew? So she practiced.

McGowan left shortly after dinner, filled with good food and a fair amount of information about Jackie's interests, hobbies, and ideas about life. Jackie carefully locked the front door behind him, and double-checked the kitchen door. She locked the door to the basement. She checked on all the window locks. While she did all of this, Peter followed her around the house, his eyes full of excitement. When at last everything was bolted and double-bolted, Jackie tucked Peter in, carried the portable telephone into his room, and went downstairs to her desk in the family room. She still wanted to look at Barger's files.

She studied them for half an hour, finding nothing. The

file folders were full of his course notes, ancient lecture notes, and ideas that had evidently never been carried out. There was nothing that referred to the Kestrel books, or to Graham Grosset.

One folder, however, intrigued her. In it was a mimeographed flyer from a series of lectures given two years ago in the Romance Languages department. Paul Cook's name had been circled; Jackie smiled. Then she sat bolt upright. "March 4, 3:00 P.M.," she read. "Room 306, Mallory Hall. Undiscovered Masters of the Portuguese Romantic Novel."

Jackie Walsh did not believe in coincidence. She reached for the phone and dialed Paul Cook. They talked for twenty minutes or so; Paul was surprised at her request, but yes, yes, he could certainly dig up his notes from that lecture. Yes, he could meet her at his office first thing tomorrow. He was glad to put them to some kind of use. This would make a grand total of four people who had been interested in the topic, he remarked, chuckling.

Make that five, thought Jackie. Five.

CHAPTER 17

Jackie arrived at Paul Cook's office early the next morning. He was leaning up against the edge of his desk, a stack of well-thumbed index cards in his hand. "What's this all about, Jackie?" he asked, handing them over.

"Murder," replied Jackie evenly. "Do you mind if I sit in here and look through them quickly?"

"Not at all, not at all." He gestured to a worn wooden armchair, and Jackie sat.

Five minutes passed. Jackie looked up. "Who's this Paolo Gilberto guy?"

"Ah. My *favorite* of the undiscovered greats. Actually, he was more of a poet than a novelist. Had a lot in common with Byron—temperamentally. Lived a wild life on a mountainside, above the coastline in Portugal, where he invited his friends to come and stay for months at a time. Wrote fantastic tales that are practically unknown outside of a few European literary circles."

"Did he write a book about a crippled architect bent on a savage type of revenge?"

Paul looked at her in surprise. "Not a book. A poem."

"Oh—right. This it—this name?" She pointed to a line on one of the index cards.

"*Francelho*. Yes, that's it."

"That a bird?"

Paul's eyes widened. "You want to share with me your secret knowledge?"

"Sure. Later. First, I think I need to talk to our illustrious visiting genius. Thank you, Paul. Don't say a word, please."

"Scout's honor."

Jackie found Graham Grosset in his office. She knocked, and he looked up, his eyes bright, his habitual look of insouciance gone.

"My dearest child," he said. "Do come right in. Right on in." He was making the effort, but Jackie could see that he was tired.

"I've come about the project. You're right. It's a bad idea. We should forget the whole thing."

Grosset brightened visibly for a moment, but Jackie's expression told him everything he needed to know. "Oh. Dear me," he said at last. "Sit down, my child, and talk to me."

Jackie sat. She felt suddenly terribly sorry for this man, who had worked so hard for so long to keep up the charade. Twenty years is a long time to pretend. "Don't you think you'd feel better if you just owned up to it?" she asked gently.

"I just *knew* you'd say that," he retorted with a vestige of his usual spark. "You Americans are so predictable, with your work ethic and your demands for openness and honesty. Really." He shook his head, pitying; then he grinned at Jackie. "But I do think I am rather tired of the whole game."

"You didn't write those books at all, did you?"

"The Kestrel books? Good heavens, yes—that is, I put them into their present form. Translated from an obscure manuscript by an obscure Portuguese rake. He was a terrible poet, dreadful. I did him a favor, really—because he was a master of invention, but his approach to storytelling was just deadly."

"And then when you won the Hodgman Prize—"

"Well, naturally it was far too late to say a word to

anyone about where the story had come from." He smiled at Jackie. "I had a feeling that you would find out my little secret."

"Dr. Grosset—two people have died."

"Well, *I* know that, my dear. But what has that to do with me?"

"Everything. But don't you know?"

"No. I know nothing, except that your talented and sophisticated Mr. Barger seems to have got his just desserts."

"Because of your project."

The blood drained from Grosset's face. "Surely not."

"I think so. He was blackmailing you, wasn't he?"

"Oh. Yes, I suppose you could call it blackmail. I didn't pay him anything, mind you—I haven't got a farthing to my name, in spite of the great success of the Kestrel trilogy. I spend it rather too quickly. Fond of antiques, and good things."

"Yes," said Jackie, understanding.

"But he wrote to me, two years ago, and said he had a proposition. Wouldn't I consider allowing him to have the movie rights, and so forth—and in exchange, he would never reveal my secret."

"And you agreed?"

"I didn't really have much choice. I was afraid that my publishers would sue me, and that everything I had would be taken away. It seemed expedient to come to America and be part of it. You mustn't fight City Hall, you know." He smiled at her.

"Who else knew about the arrangements between you and Barger?"

"Oh, great heavens, no one. That was part of our deal. I was *most particular* about that. Most particular, indeed."

"You may have been particular, Dr. Grosset," said Jackie, "but I don't think Barger kept his end up." She sat, lost in thought, for a moment.

"Please—don't keep me in suspense any longer, my dear.

What fell plans have you for me, now that you know the grim truth?"

"I have no plans, Dr. Grosset. At the moment, however, I am afraid that your life may be in danger. We have a homicidal nut loose at Rodgers." She stood up to go. "What about *The Tale of Gorgonzola*?"

"Ah. Now, *that* is entirely my own."

"Glad to hear it," said Jackie. "It's my favorite."

"Yes, well—I knew you had taste, my dear."

"Look after yourself, won't you?" She departed, feeling altogether sad.

Jackie stopped in at the Longacre Center briefly, to put up a notice canceling her class for the day. She didn't stop to collect her mail and messages from her pigeonhole, but headed straight for home. She wanted to look again at Barger's notes, which were still on her desk in the study. This was why she didn't know that Paul Cook had telephoned, leaving a message for her to call him back. Urgent, said Paul's message.

Jake greeted Jackie with all the enthusiasm he could muster. In spite of his somewhat advanced years and unusual personal history, he was still very much a dog; and he didn't relish the long hours that he was obliged to spend at home by himself, waiting for Peter and Jackie to return. He settled himself at Jackie's feet while she read through the folders once more.

Barger had made notes about his discovery, Jackie found. They were rather cryptic memoranda, each no more than a paragraph or two, that had been dictated to Polly Merton over a period of three or four months. In one, Barger mentioned that the foreign office had been contacted; in another, that the foreign sale had been outlined; in a third, that the foreign sale had been consummated.

And on each one of them, at the bottom, was a note, in Barger's hand: "bcc: MG."

Jackie was so deeply absorbed in her findings that she didn't hear, at first, the footsteps on the front stoop. Jake heard them, however, and rushed to the front hall. Jackie rose, went to the door, and peered out through the small spyglass.

Merida Green was on the doorstep.

Jackie's heart thudded, and she took a step back, toward the kitchen. The telephone. And then, with a mounting sense of horror, she saw the handle of the front door turn. She had forgotten to lock the front door. She was trapped.

"Might as well be hung for a sheep as a lamb," she said to herself. She took three steps, turned the doorknob, and pulled the door open.

"Merida! What brings you here?" Jake growled. "Hush, boy, it's okay." Jackie opened the door wide. "Come on in." Jackie looked over Merida's shoulder to see if there was anyone on the street—anyone at all who might have seen the woman arrive. But the street was deserted.

Merida Green stepped into the front hall and turned to Jackie. There was a strange light in her eyes, and her lips were very dry.

"Maybe I can save you the trouble, Merida," said Jackie. "You came to talk to me about Philip, didn't you? And Danielle?"

Without a word, Merida drew a small gun from her handbag. She nodded at Jake. "Get rid of the dog."

"He's a very good dog, he won't hurt you. Old, too," said Jackie. "Not a threat. Not to worry. Put the gun away, Merida."

"Shut up," said Merida. She turned the gun on Jake.

"Don't do that, Merida."

"Shut up," said the woman. She aimed the gun.

"Get her, Jake," said Jackie.

In the blink of an eye, Jake attacked with all the fury and savagery in his nature. The gun clattered to the floor, and before ten seconds were up, Merida Green was pinned to the floor, her face a mask of horror. Jake stood over her, his paws on her shoulders, his pointed teeth bared. He snarled quietly, with vicious authority.

Jackie ran to the kitchen and called Michael McGowan.

CHAPTER 18

In Jackie and Peter's kitchen, Cosmo Gordon and Michael McGowan listened, transfixed, to the story of Merida's capture. She had been taken away, several hours before, by the same young policewoman who had been so skeptical of Jackie's intruder the other night. Jackie hadn't been able to resist a smirk when the woman had turned up again in her kitchen.

Peter listened eagerly, now certain that he not only had the finest mom, but also the finest dog, in the world. Isaac would never top this one. He sat on the floor, proudly stroking Jake's fur, while Jackie, still running on an adrenaline high, described the moment of Jake's attack.

Lieutenant McGowan had spent four hours taking down Merida Green's confession. He related the details of it now, briefly.

"She and Barger were in on the Grosset deal from the start. It was she, not Barger, who first found out that Grosset's material wasn't original; and she went to Paul Cook's lecture to see if her idea was right. He didn't talk about *Francelho*— whatever it's called—because it's a poem, evidently."

"Right," said Jackie.

"But Merida Green asked him about it, later. When the lecture was over."

"And he remembered that this afternoon," said Jackie. "That's why he tried to reach me at the office. And Merida, naturally, must have read his message. She's such

173

a snoop—always reading everyone's mail and messages. Those pigeonholes have got to go."

"What about the young woman?" asked Gordon. "Danielle Sherman."

"Oh, I think she had figured it out," said McGowan. "She had worked out that somehow Barger was cutting Grosset out of the film profits entirely. So she decided to ask for a piece of the action."

"And?"

"And Barger, most likely, told her to go jump in a lake."

Jackie nodded to herself. The couple had "broken up."

McGowan continued. "But when Barger turned up dead, Danielle put two and two together. She had probably read the files, and knew that there had been someone else involved originally—Merida Green. The two of them, according to Merida Green's confession, had cooked up the plan together. But when Grosset had agreed to it, Barger had cut the Green woman out of the deal—leaving her hopping mad and hell-bent on revenge, if I'm any judge. She was something else this afternoon."

Cosmo Gordon looked thoughtfully toward Peter. "Young man" he began, "perhaps—"

Peter, sensing what was coming, appealed instantly to his mother. "I can stay, Mom, can't I?"

"I think so, Petey." She smiled at Gordon. "It's better if we all know the truth, don't you think? Better than letting our imaginations go haywire." She turned to McGowan. "Details, please, Michael."

McGowan obliged with further details. Apparently, Merida Green had hatched her plan a long time ago; she had merely waited until the moment seemed right to carry it out. According to McGowan, she already had a clandestine duplicate of the key to the editing lab—which she had made not with murder in mind, but because it offended her sense of self-importance not to have one. The night she killed Barger, she had in fact attended the Women in Film meeting—there were hundreds of witnesses. But she had simply slipped away right after delivering her speech; Merida Green knew from experience that nobody would notice her absence from the cocktail reception afterward. She had driven back to Palmer, which was only an hour, really, from Boston, if you weren't afraid to do seventy-five on the Turnpike. Then she had gone to the Longacre Center for a prearranged confrontation with Barger.

"I guess he behaved like a real jerk," said McGowan. "She went there ready to tangle with him, and he just smirked at her."

Jackie felt a chill run up her spine. She had seen that smirk of Barger's often enough to know how infuriating it could be. The man really almost had it coming to him, she thought. He had been very careless about making enemies.

"So Merida Green asked to be cut into the deal," McGowan went on. "She told him she wanted to handle the screenplay. Apparently she'd seen what he'd done, and knew it would never work. There was a lot more money to be made from a successful film, naturally."

"*I'll* say Barger's script wouldn't work," concurred Jackie, a faint sparkle in her eyes. "It's the pits."

McGowan continued with his tale. Barger had laughed at Merida Green. Venomously angry, and determined to reap the rewards—monetary and otherwise—of the *Kestrel* project, she put her plan into action. She waited until Barger turned his back, then slipped the poison in his drink and departed. "She went back to her own office to wait it out," said McGowan, as though such a simple explanation was an everyday thing.

"Unbelievable," said Jackie. "I knew she had nerves, but I didn't know they were made of steel."

"You mean to say she just sat in her office, waiting?" asked Gordon, protest in his voice.

"Yup," said McGowan, nodding. "She knew it wouldn't take long." He glanced at Jackie. "She took your note for Polly."

"And then she dragged the body down the hall? She must be quite an athlete." Gordon looked disbelieving.

"Built like an Amazon," concurred McGowan, with an appraising look at Jackie. "She would have been more than a match for you, Jackie, even without her gun."

"Not for *Jake*, though," put in Peter proudly.

"No," agreed Gordon, "Jake's not met his match yet." He gave McGowan a look, which the others missed.

Jackie was shaking her head. "Danielle had left all the answers for me. In her midterm—she knew it was risky to take on Merida Green. When that exam disappeared from my office today, I should have known at once that Merida had taken it. She had been so insistent on having copies of all those papers, and she terrified me into handing them over to the department secretary. But of course, I didn't hand over Danielle's. And so she came and took it."

Gordon was still curious about the mechanics of the murder and its aftermath. "Michael, how did Grosset get his hands on the manuscript? I thought he was the guilty one, I'll admit—especially when that screenplay turned up in his hands."

"Merida Green sent it to him," replied McGowan simply.

"She *what*!?" Jackie was really incensed. It was bad enough that the woman was a murderer, but she had compounded her offenses severely by allowing Jackie to waste endless hours with Stuart Goodwillie, B. Crowder Westfall, the sneering Polly Merton, and—above all—Harmless Henry Obermaier. Really, that had been adding insult to injury. Jackie felt her face grow hot with anger. "She knew where it was all along? That—" Jackie stifled her comment.

"Afraid so," put in McGowan, with a civil servant's sympathy for the frustrations of political maneuvering.

"Never mind that," ordered Gordon gruffly. "Why on earth did she send it to him?"

"To let him know that the game was still afoot," suggested Jackie. Michael McGowan nodded his acknowledgment.

"I think so. No safer place for it, really—and of course she sent it anonymously. But a creative and determined killer, I'd say. She'd probably have killed Grosset, if she had thought it would make things run more smoothly for her. Kill anybody who got in her way." He looked at Jackie, who was staring thoughtfully at the floor.

"I didn't read Danielle's midterm," she said, looking up at last, "but Merida must have thought I had. That's why she came here today." She attempted a smile. "Well. At least I don't need to worry about intruders anymore. I'm not surprised she brought a gun the second time the way Jake carried on on Sunday night."

McGowan and Gordon exchanged looks. Jackie picked up on it. "What? What are you saying?" she demanded.

"Mrs. Walsh," said Gordon quietly, "that wasn't Merida Green out there the other night."

"No?" Jackie felt the panic begin to rise again. "Of course it was. Who else would it be?" She took Peter's hand, and with her foot felt under the table for the reassuring warmth of Jake's fur.

McGowan shook his head. "No, Jackie," he said softly. "Merida Green didn't know, until this afternoon, that you could implicate her. She didn't know until she saw Danielle Sherman's exam paper."

"So." Jackie tried to sound upbeat. "It was just a regular old burglar then, the first time. Whew. I feel much better."

"There's something I think you ought to know," replied Gordon. He told her, briefly and cogently, about Matt Dugan's death. "He wasn't a very good cop, Mrs. Walsh, but he was my friend. And he was Jake's friend."

"And?"

"He had stumbled onto something. A scandal, he told me, in the highest ranks of Palmer politics. I dismissed it, I'm afraid to say. I didn't listen to him. But I got a call from the boys in ballistics the other day. The bullet that killed Matt Dugan was fired from a gun known to us

from previous crimes. Mob-related shootings. I think Matt
was onto something."

"Well what has this got to do with us? With me and
Peter?"

"Nothing to do with you. Everything, however, to do
with the dog." Gordon spoke quietly but firmly.

"Oh." Jackie gulped.

"I think you might be better off if you were to give him
up, Mrs. Walsh."

"No! No *way*!" shouted Peter. He was on his feet in a
flash. "Forget it, just forget it, you—"

"Peter!" Jackie spoke as sharply as she knew how. "You're
forgetting your manners. Sit down and be quiet, or you'll
have to leave the room."

Peter, his eyes filling swiftly with tears, did as he was
told. His mother almost never spoke to him that way; when
she did, she meant business.

Jackie returned her attention to Gordon. "I think not,"
she said quietly.

"But Mrs. Walsh—"

"No." She looked at Jake. "That dog saved my life
today."

"But, Jackie—" McGowan protested.

"No. Absolutely not."

"They'll be back, Mrs. Walsh," said Gordon.

"They? Do you know who they are?"

"The police are working on it," Gordon replied, his tone
full of dissatisfaction. "But Michael and I have talked it
over. We're afraid that whoever is responsible may come
back here, to get the dog. He was there, you see, at the time
of the shooting."

"Jake, you're a *witness!*" exclaimed Peter.

"Of sorts," Gordon agreed. He looked at Jackie, who
clearly had no intention of yielding the point. The dog
would stay.

"Then we'll just have to be extra careful of the dog, Dr.
Gordon," she said. "Maybe Jake will be able to help. I

think, after all, that we might be able to help him crack his big case. Right, Petey?"

"Right, Mom."

"So." Jackie spoke firmly to McGowan. "We'll be here, Peter and Jake and I, when you need our help. I think we owe Jake that much, don't you?" She smiled at Peter, who smiled back. The best mom, and the best dog, in the world.

"We'll find the guy, Jake," said Peter to the dog. "And when we do, we'll let you at him."

Jake looked up at Peter, blinked, and yawned. It would be all in a day's work.

A *Romance* FOR EVERY MOOD™

JUST CAN'T GET ENOUGH?

Join our social communities
and talk to us online.

You will have access to the latest
news on upcoming titles and special
promotions, but most importantly,
you can talk to other fans about your
favorite Harlequin reads.

Harlequin.com/Community

 Facebook.com/HarlequinBooks

 Twitter.com/HarlequinBooks

 Pinterest.com/HarlequinBooks

HSOCIAL

Turn your love of reading into rewards you'll love with

Harlequin My Rewards

Join for FREE today at www.HarlequinMyRewards.com

Earn **FREE BOOKS** of your choice.

Experience **EXCLUSIVE OFFERS** and contests.

Enjoy **BOOK RECOMMENDATIONS** selected just for you.

PLUS! Sign up now and get **500** points right away!

Earn **FREE** REWARDS Join Today! HarlequinMyRewards.com

MYR16R